It was a dark night at the two-story, subur.
Wisconsin home of John Anderson and his dau
on Park-view Drive. Up past her usual bedt.
knees, elbows propped up against the pink b:
sized bed. The room, painted with cute chil. ....gs and iv snow
posters and other miscellaneous items, also was a sanctum for the
lonely girl. Each and every night, she asked God for her father's
health, as well as to have a good life and other things; being a
little kid, some of what she asked for included a game system, a
new bike, etc. But for the most part, she wished for the good life
she'd always dreamed of.

  John knocked on the door to Sarah's room. Seeing that she was
  still up, he frowned upon entering. "Sarah, I thought I said it
  was your bedtime almost an hour ago" demanded her father.

  "I'm sorry dad.." she said, finished praying. "I was just
  praying."

  John smiled. "Is that so? Why are you praying?"

  "I just want to make sure mommy is happy, and to see if she
  could watch and protect me.

John grinned. "Well, in the way of making people know your point.
Acts of kindness, I'm not so sure."

  "Da-ad," Sarah whined and eventually started pouting as John
  laughed.

  "All right, hurry up, get to bed" he said, while he stood in her
  bedroom doorway.

  "Dad, do you think God can hear my prayers?" Sarah questioned.

  John turned back to his beautiful little girl, replying, "Of
  course, my dear, and your guardian angel will too." She sat
  there curious as can be. Of course, John noticed the look on
  her face, so he took the liberty to further explain.

  "A guardian angel is an angel that watches over you to protect
  you and, sometimes, even heals you a time of need."

  "How do you get your guardian angel?" she asked.

  "By looking at the stars in the sky and asking for a guardian
  angel. If you get a yes, one of the stars will shine brightly
  but only you will see it." He saw the eagerness in her eyes.
  Sarah had to have everything, but having a guardian angel, she
  wanted most of all.

  . It seemed like a worthy dream to chase.

She continued to pray very softly for quite some time and at last, she whispered amen. One could hear the hope in her voice. Once that she finished her prayer, she didn't know what to do. She should have also prayed for more patience, because she couldn't bare to wait any longer. She even began to beleive the story wasn't true, but she held fast to her faith.

Before she knew it, she saw a special star and knew that her guardian angel had answered her prayers. It was shining so brightly, but John couldn't see it, only she could.

What a cute little kid.

Chapter 1

Chase, what are you doing?"

The young dark angel barely even heard his best friend, Jackson. He looked at the girl with a passion, a father might have when he looked at his newborn baby for the first time. She had long straight dirty blonde hair, and chocolate-brown eyes. Her face thinned at the jaw, and she had a small cute nose above small lips.

"I feel like she the one to protect though" Chase said.

Jackson rolled his eyes. "Okay, just because you're the perfect match for you, I don't think God will approve of you."

Chase turned around quickly. "What do you mean? I know everything about taking care of the one I protect!"

"Well" Jackson turned thoughtful, "we know what will happen to her, and we have to do everything we can to stop or lessen the pain. You...well you won't protect her. You will treat her like your child, and forget about your job. Your just too emotional."

"What do you mean?" Chase asked angrily.

Jackson sighed. "You're a dark angel. You were allowed into heaven because of your good deeds and because you are a believer. But you still kept your emotions and pain, and the ability to die."

"So?"

"So dark angels are never allowed to be guardian angels. They can't handle it. The last dark angel who was a guardian angel sacrificed his life to save his child, and he vanished, like he never existed. Then the one before that was even worse."

Chase perked up. "Who was that one?"

"He was the first, and half the reason dark angels can't be guardians."

Chase got impatient. "I didn't ask-"

"Satan."

Chase went silent in surprise. Satan? "You mean the devil?" When Jackson nodded, Chase asked "how?"

"...let me tell you the story..."

"Way back in time, you know that Satan was God's right hand man, an angel. But, a dark angel. No one ever knew how he became a darkies, but God knew he would turn evil. That was when he created hell. He assigned Satan to a young woman, named Eve. Eve was pure of heart, but within a week, he had made her think differently, an exploring mind, a rebellious personality, though somehow he could not corrupt her heart. He made her eat the apple of knowledge. Eve was punished because she couldn't resist temptation, but Satan was cast into hell. He has tried to overtake Heaven ever since."

"So I can't be a guardian because of the devil and some idiot who threw his life away?"

Jackson grinned. "Well the idiot is a lot like you."

Chase huffed. "Well I will go and be the guardian angel for this girl."

Jackson smiled. "Good luck!"

Early the next morning, Sarah heard a loud knock on the front door. Her father was at work and she was home alone. Man, I have homework to do, school on monday, plus I have to call Samantha. So who could be at the door. People rarely visited her early in the morning. Like all girls, she had questions, but unlike all girls, she began to worry and overexagerated.

Thought such as what if it's a robber? or what if someone is here to kidnap me? and even I might have to call the police. entered her mind.

She had to remind herself it wasn't that dramatic, and she just had to answer it. It can't be that bad she thought to herself.

Hesitantly, Sarah tiptoed to the front door. She opened the door, but no one was there. "Hello?" she shouted. Not a sound, not even the noise of her neighbors annoying Yorkies. In the midst of shutting the door, an unfamiliar voice said " Hello, how are you Sarah? It's great to finally meet you."

Quickly, Sarah whipped around to see a strange man at the door. He appeared out of nowhere! At first Sarah just stood there, awestruck by the handsome young man. He had messy short black hair, and beautiful light blue eyes. It wasn't a huge surprise to see him, as he seemed familiar. But then, she began to freak out.

" What the" she yelled "Where did you? Who are you?"

He tried to calm her down. "Look I'm just" but she continued to yell. "Who are you and how do you know my name!?!

"Well you did ask for a guardian angel." Sarah gave the angel a quizzical look. "But how did you know that" Sarah questioned. This was getting freaky.

"Because I heard from heaven asking someone to protect you. I wanted the job since you seem like a nice girl, so here I am!" explained the angel.

"Give me a minute." said Sarah. This was really getting freaky. I actually got an angel! She had prayed and prayed for something good, and now she got it. But this was too weird. She had faith in her fathers words, so it wasn't too bad. But the angel was...different than she imagined. He wore a dark grey trench coat, and black pants, and converse shoes. And he had a glow, not a white one, but a blue one.

After her requested minute, she asked "So your my guarding angel." It was more a rhetorical question, but the angel answered anyway. "Yeah" he said.

' Well that's amazing and all, and I really am astounded and grateful, but i thought angels had wings?"

"We do but their invisible said chase." "Sweet can i ask you a question said Sarah?

How old are you asked Sarah as she playing with her hair.

"Sure" said Chase with a grin. "I am 16 years old, but technically, in heaven, I'm 108 years old."

Sarah's jaw dropped. 108! That means he's been dead for 92 years! She wondered what it was like in heaven. She voiced this question, and Chase said "it's pretty amazing. You can do WHATEVER you want" he said with happiness, emphasizing the whatever. "As long as it makes you happy and it's not evil."

Sarah pictured this in her mind. She imagined herself skiing, playing Xbox 360, riding horses, being with her boyfriend or husband, everything she could imagine. It was a great dream.

"Well, I am a dark angel, and I am also the angel of the Lord" said Chase . "So...what is that?" asked Sarah with a questioning look on her face.

Chase scratched his chin. "Um, I protect you and go on a mission for God" explained Chase. "Oh, ok..." she looked at Chase with interest. He defiantly isn't normal she thought humorously. She thought he looked very cute and...odd. "Uh, do you know when my dad gets here? asked Sarah.

A door-slamming sounded right outside the house.

"Now!" said Chase with a smirk on his face. Sarah smiled and went to the door. "You should hide. My dad won't like someone older than me being here." she looked over to Chase, still grinning. "I don't think he'll mind."

"Hey, sweetie I'm home yelled John as he entered the house door. His hair and clothes was drenched from the rain, and he shook his head like a dog before looking up to see a boy in a black coat and jeans.

"Hey, dad meet my new friend!" said Sarah nervously holding her white t-shirt. "Hey, Mr. Anderson, my name Chase Archer" Chase introduced himself, as if he wasn't worried. He held out his hand to the man.

"Well, hello." said John, shaking the stranger's hand with a questioning look on his face. "Can I ask you what you're doing here with my daughter?"

Chase shrugged. "Actually, I was here to visit you, you know, introduce myself. I'm new here and I heard you were good people. Your daughter is a very nice host, I might add."

John nodded. "Okay, well then it's nice to meet you, uh, Chase." He turned to Sarah. "Um...sweetie! How was your day?" asked the still concerned father.

"I didn't do much until Chase came around." said Sarah. John grinned. "Well thank you, Chase, for entertaining my daughter for me" said John. "I actually had a hard day at work, so..." "Not a problem" Chase replied, laughing a little. The mysterious angel turned to look at Sarah.

John clasped his hands together. "Chase are you hungry?" asked John "We are having steak tonight, a young man like yourself couldn't pass up some nice and well-cooked meat?" Chase held up a hand, "Nah, I'm not hungry. Besides, I have to get going soon." John shrugged. "Alright. Sarah, we'll have dinner in a bit, the steak has marinated for a while so it shouldn't be too long. Chase" he looked at the respectful young man "take care, will you?" He took one last look at Chase, nodded and smiled, then went into the kitchen whist taking his coat off on the way.

"Chase...are you leaving me?" whispered Sarah. "No, I'm just going to be invisible to your father. Trust me, all will be clear to you one day" Chase reassured her. Sarah had a weird look on her face because her guardian angel didn't open his mouth to speak. She actually heard his voice...in her head. Chase noticed the look and said "It's telepathy, where I can talk to you in your mind instead

of out-loud. In a while, you will be able too, but only with me."
Sarah nodded, understanding "Oh" she said in her mind, hoping that
chase heard her. He smiled but said nothing.

"Now I will be with you the whole time, but act as if I'm not,
okay?." he explained. "OK then. Do what you have to do." said
Sarah with a sigh. Chase closed his eyes and put his hands in the
air, moving them ever so slightly, while doing a weird chant.
"Onggee soulee nov." Sarah couldn't tell the effects of what he
did but when he was done he opened his eyes and stared at Sarah
with his light blue eyes.

Confused, Sarah tried to ask "What did you do?" But her father
interrupted her thoughts.

"Sarah, time for dinner!"

With questions buzzing in her head, she walked towards the
kitchen, her strange Guardian Angel in tow.

"So, Sarah what do you know about this Chase guy?" asked the STILL
concerned father, John Anderson.

"Nothing too much, he didn't tell me much" Sarah replied, a little
annoyed. I just KNOW the rest of this dinner will be a Q&A.

John looked at his daughter with interest, knowing she was getting
angry, aggravated, annoyed, or stressed. But he wanted to make
sure his daughter was safe...he didn't want some boy taking away
his girl.

"Where did he go?" John asked. "He went home to his...... father,
on Ricky Lane. A two-story house at the base" explained Sarah. "At
least, that's what he said. She looked nervously over at Chase who
was leaning against the wall. The Angel looked at the young woman
with a dark look in his eyes.

John leaned in on the table, his stomach rubbing against the china plate. "U-huh. Why do you know that, honey? Tell me why you know where this teenage boy lives."

Thinking fast, she said "He just wanted me to know so that if we wanted to hang out, or, um, if me and you wanted to visit him and his dad, we could" she lied. "Your pretty good at lying. Chase's voice rang in her head. Too bad it's a sin." Sarah glared over to where Chase stood, grinning. John looked over to see a wall. He looked questioningly at Sarah but decided not to pursue the matter.

"Oh, alright then" he said, "Maybe we should visit him sometime." When Sarah shrugged, he decided to move on to his next question. "So do you know what Chase's father does?" asked John. Sarah threw her hands up and said "why would that matter?" John shrugged. "I just want to know."

He's suspicious Sarah thought. She had to think of something quick. She could change the subject, or make something up. Then she came up with a brilliant idea. "He's in the army."

"His father is in the army now and he is the captain or commander in Iraq" said Sarah. I'm good she thought proudly before looking over to see Chase giving her an exasperated stare and whispered 'why'. Once again, John looked over to the same spot of the wall, and only saw a painting of The Last Supper. Maybe she is still thinking about the angel thing I told her about a while ago he thought. Yeah, that must be it.

Oh, Sarah. Do you have Chase's number?" asked John. No he doesn't have one." Sarah said. Technically, she was telling the truth. "All kids at his age have cell phones!" commented John. "What does that mean? Maybe he can't afford one!" Sarah said, thinking she had turned the tables on her father. "I saw his clothes. Trust me, he has enough money to have a cell phone." Sarah deflated. She tried to make something else up.

"Well his father can't get one now but can we get him one and maybe new clothes too?" asked Sarah. What? Chase asked in her mind. It will make you seem more real! If you don't like it, then you shouldn't have shown your face! John looked at his daughter carefully. "Now why should I do that? He has clothes, and I think he can afford a cell. So why?"

Sarah shrugged. "I don't know, I just think he needs some help right now!"

John sighed. "Look, honey, we don't have the money to go and buy your friends clothes and phones. I'm sure he will be fine. Now go get ready for bed, it's almost 10, and you have school tomorrow."

John got up and took his and Sarah's used dishes to the kitchen. "I'll do the dishes for you." John said with a smile. Sarah hugged her father. "Thanks, Dad. Goodnight."

"Goodnight, sweetie." John said, doing his best to hug her back. They broke the embrace and headed their separate ways.

"Hey, Chase."

Sarah entered her clean room. She turned on her light only so she could ask a few questions to Chase.

"Yeah?" he said, following her into the room. He gazed at it for a few seconds, looking at Sarah's daily life. Average room, except for the crosses and prayers on the walls, and the bible on her desk.

"Why were you invisible to my dad? Why couldn't he see you?"

Chase laughed. "Oh, well that's something I can do. Remember the weird chant I did?" Sarah nodded. "Well that makes me visible only to you. Normally, you are the only person that can see me and touch me, but I can make it so I seem alive and so other people can interact with me. It's a simple process, really."

Sarah nodded. She was getting used to his weird abilities. "Oh, ok. Thanks for the demo!" Sarah joked. There was a knock at the door "Come in!" said Sarah.

"Are you praying?" asked John as he held the door slightly ajar.

"No" Sarah replied while getting into bed. "Alright, just wanted to say goodnight." said John.

"Uh, goodnight Dad" said Sarah as John kissed her on the cheek and hugged her. "I'm be getting a little old for that" Sarah said. John grinned.

He was about to leave, but Sarah still had a question. "Dad?" asked Sarah as she lay in bed.

What, Sarah?" John turned to Sarah halfway through the doorway.

'Can you tell me about how mom left?"

'No, Sarah. Another time." John said firmly.

'Please? I deserve to know!" said Sarah, a bit loudly, holding her hands together. John sighed and walked over to sit on Sarah's bed. 'Alright, fine! I will tell you about your mother" John said slowly and gravely...

Sarah sat on her bed, on the verge of tears. John's arm was around her shoulders. Chase was sadly looking at the girl. Her mother had been hit by a car, and her body was very much broken. The driver was one of Sarah's older friends too, and he was intoxicated.

"I'm sorry sweetie. I guess I should have told you earlier," John said sympathetically. "No, I'm glad she didn't die too terribly," Sarah sobbed. "I do appreciate you telling me dad."

John smiled warmly. "Get some sleep. You will feel better in the morning."

Sarah nodded. John left the room, and Chase took his place. "You all right?" he asked.

"Yeah, it's good he told me now. Before, I would have taken it really badly." Chase nodded. "I understand. I have to go now, and your father is right. Get some sleep."

Chapter 2- Invisible Angel

A loud beeping noise screamed in Sarah's ear. Still tired, she tried to ignore the sound. But after 5 or 10 minutes, it was still going, so Sarah turned and slapped the snooze button on her alarm clock. She sat up and yawned. Rubbing her eyes, she looked around for her guardian angel. He wasn't anywhere. Maybe I imagined it she thought? Pushing those thoughts aside, she glanced at the time. 7:42. Realizing today was monday, she got up, and prepared to go to school.

The thoughts of her mother ran through her head. She knew this was going to be a problem.

She brushed her teeth, put on a shirt, vest, and jeans. Then she put her weekend homework on her desk in her bag, picked up her cell phone, and walked downstairs. She glanced into her fathers room. Gone. He must be working a 24-hour shift she told herself.

Preparing her bag of school supplies, she book her bag on the table and poured a bowl of Coco Puffs.

As she munched on the chocolate treat, she thought of her school schedule today. Mrs. Shire for math first, then Mr. Shanken for history, Mr. Erikson for biology...and then lunch...okay, then I

think Ms. York for health and to finish Mr. Karrole to end the day
with english. Geez..I hope I don't have a run in Mr. Reinhart she
thought with a shudder. She finished her Coco puffs and put her
bowl in the dishwasher. Quickly wiping her mouth with a napkin,
she grabbed her bag and walked down the street.

The school was only 15 blocks away and it was her daily way of
staying physically fit. Sarah got used to the walk and actually
enjoyed it. Sometimes she would see some energetic young men do
parkour around the neighborhood. Although it looked cool when
they hopped between houses, there was no way she would do
anything of that sort.

After a short 5 block walk, she heard walking suddenly behind her.
She turned around as normal as possible without appearing scared.
She jumped when she saw who it was.

"Hey, Sarah," said Chase with his usual grin.

"Oh my God, you scared me!" Sarah said loudly. She continued
walking, with Chase walking silently next to her. "Where are you
going?" he asked.

Sarah rolled her eyes. "School obviously. I assume you'll be
joining me?" Chase nodded. "And you will be invisible?" He nodded
again. "Great." She said a little sarcastically.

Chase looked at her closely. "I think" he began, "I hear a little
tone!"

"Well your going to be a distraction from my schoolwork, I'm
sure!"

'Don't worry! I won't bother you, but I will just bother somebody
else," said Chase smiling.

Sarah sighed. "Well this is going to be just wonderful!"

"I thought you wanted a guardian angel." Chase said, a little
hurt. "I do, and I'm glad your here, but you are a little
too...YOU for me to do my schoolwork properly. But we can still
have fun!" Sarah explained.

"Alright let's have some fun." Chase said cheerily.

"Don't get me into trouble," Sarah warned him with a very serious
face.

"I won't" Chase assured her as he followed Sarah to her school.

The school was 2 stories high, made of blue colored stone walls.
Kids and teens were entering the middle school already, mumbling
amongst themselves. The weekend was over and nobody liked it.
Sarah felt the same.

"Cheer up!" said Chase, putting his hands on his hips. "It'll be more fun now that I'm here!" Sarah rolled her eyes.

They walked inside and headed to Sarah's locker. Kids seemed to walk through Chase, and when they did Chase giggled a little. When Sarah asked the boy how he did this, Chase explained it tickled a little. Reaching her locker, Sarah dumped some of her school supplies in and took out her math, history, and biology book. Taking 3 notebooks, a calculator, and a few pens and pencils, she closed her locker and walked to the math room.

Chase followed Sarah into her classroom and he leaned up against the wall, while Sarah sat in the first row in the middle. Other kids were talking amongst themselves, and some greeted Sarah as she sat down. Soon, an older looking woman with long brown hair entered the room.

"Alright class," Mrs.Shire announced in a clear voice. "Let's go over your homework!"

Ugh Sarah she heard Chase say in her thoughts. Sarah smirked and flipped open her notebook that had 1-33 titled on the top. She had to do questions 1-33 (page 229), obviously, on factors.

As the teacher droned on about the homework and lesson review, with Sarah absentmindedly checking the questions she got wrong (not too many, about a B worth paper), Sarah watched Chase sitting as he stared at the Numbers posters (a T.V show). Chase meanwhile rolled up some gum, and Sarah presumed someone would have it in his or her hair soon.

At last the teacher finished the homework review, and she gave them another assignment on page 230-234 1-10, 15-30, 34, 36, 41-46.

As the class did their homework Sarah heard Chase whisper in her mind.

Hey Sarah, watch this. Suddenly, a piece of white chalk was flying through the air at the teacher.

The chalk puffed against her head. A couple students chuckled, but Mrs. Shire wasn't amused. "Who did that?!" yelled the teacher. She looked at the entire class and saw 'little Micheal' (a nickname given to Micheal Weren't who was 4'3" tall) sitting closest to the chalk. "Micheal to the Principle's office, NOW!" Mrs. Shire screamed, pointing towards the door.

"But i didn't do it!", complained Michael. "Now!" yelled Mrs. Shire.

Everyone watched Michael leave the room and then after he left, they continued to do their work.

"I can't believe you did that chase", said sarah. "Relax - I'll be back" said Chase.

Sarah blinked and when she opened her eyes, he was gone.

Five minutes later, Chase appeared back to the same corner with a smile on his face.

Michael came back with a smile on his face too. "Michael I thought I told you to go the office?" asked Mrs.Shire.

"I did, but principal Reinhart believed me", said Micheal. "Why?" asked Mrs. Shire crossing her arms.

"Because, he told me he saw the whole thing when he walked by", said Michael. Sarah knew chase had done something but she couldn't figure out what it was.

"Ok, then go back to your seat", said Mrs. Shire sitting back down.

Michael went back to his seat and continued on his homework.

An hour went by and the classroom bell rang and Sarah put her math homework in her bag and then she grabbed her history book for class. Mr. Shanken, (who had brown hair and green eyes). Sarah was daydreaming in class while the others were learning about WW-11. The next class was biology with Mr. Erikson (who had dark black hair and blue eyes).

"Alright class, today we are going to analyze the breakdown of DNA and cloning". While Mr. Erickson was teaching the class, Chase knocked down one of the beakers off the table. The crash was loud and commanded immediate attention from everyone.

"What happened Rachel?" asked Mr.Erickson looking at the mess on the floor.

"I don't know" said Rachael confused. "Well don't touch it, I'll get someone to clean this up", said Mr. Erickson getting the phone.

"Chase no more breaking things!", yelled Sarah. "Promise" said Chase. Chase went over to the thermostat and turned the dial down. "Nice", thought Sarah doing her homework.

In about 10 minutes sarah felt cold. "Mr. Erickson called Aaron".

"Yes", Aaron said as Mr.Erickson turned around. "Can you turn up the temperature please? I am cold," asked Aaron.

Yes no wonder it's 60 degrees in here said Mr.Erickson. Thank you said aaron.

"Alright class let's read our answer said Mr.Erickson". After they read there answer the bell rang and it was time for lunch.

Sarah got her pizza for lunch with corn and chocolate milk and went outside to the bleaches were the other kids ate their lunch.

"Hey, what are you eating chase asked as he sit down beside her". Pizza asked sarah.

"Thats good" said chase. "Yeah" said sarah. "Ok, well i gotta go be careful", said chase standing up to leave.

"Where are you going"? asked sarah. "I have to get a truck and a cell phone...whatever they are!" said Chase.

Oh sorry and a cell phone is like the ones that hang up on the wall in the house but we came up with better idea said sarah".

"Oh ok then, well- bye" said chase". "Bye!" said sarah as she grab bed her milk and Chase was gone.

Sarah look around and couldn't find Chase. He disappeared in a matter of seconds. "How does he do that"? thought Sarah.

After a long day at school sarah got all of her homework of english vocab, and then math.

Sarah walked out of the school and saw chase by the High school .

"Hey", said chase. "Hi! How are you?" asked sarah". "Ok i guess", said Chase. Sarah yelled as Lilly was running towards her.

"Sarah, you dropped your cell phone-here, I found it by the gym door"! " And- who is this?" asked Lilly. Sarah looked at Chase and came up with an idea.

"He's my cousin from California said Sarah". "Thanks Sarah!", she heard in her head from Chase.

"Oh- well... hi my name is Lilly, and yours?"

" It's Chase Archer" he said annoyed.

"Well then hi, Sarah do you need a ride home?" asked Lilly. Before Sarah could say anything, Chase spoke.

"No- she's riding home with me!" "Oh, you drive?" asked Lilly.

"Yeah, see that Black 1967 Chevrolet Impala?" he said proudly to the shiny car.

"Wow! That's beautiful!" said Lilly. " Thanks, we gotta go!" he said looking at Sarah. "Bye Chase", Sarah said as Lilly walked away.

"Bye" said Sarah. "Come on let's go!" sarah said as she and chase made their way towards the car.

"Chase where did you go and where did you get that car?" asked Sarah.

"At the used car lot down the street. And -I also bought an iPhone and a house because that's what you told your dad," said Chase.

"I am sorry, I was trying to help, where did you get the money for all that stuff?" asked Sarah". "My Father's bank account!" said Chase. "Ok sorry, I was just curious!" said sarah. "It's fine, sorry for the confusion." said Chase.

"I forgive you. Come on and take me home." said sarah as she headed toward the Impala".

Chase parked his car in front of the house and said goodbye to sarah. "You're not coming?" asked sarah.

"No, I have to go back to heaven and then I'll be back. No screaming okay Sarah? said chase.

"I won't!" Sarah said as she waved good bye to Chase as he drove off in his shiny car. Sarah went inside to call her dad but then she realized that he was working late so she took out her books and got out a snack to eat.

She was doing her homework when she heard Chase' voice saying "here i come" in her head.

Sarah was startled when Chase appeared in the kitchen. It was something she knew she wouldn't be able to get used to.

"Hey, think you could give me some kind of warning from now on?" Chase just smiled and said: "So how's your homework coming along and i did?"

"Almost done" Sarah said with a sigh.

Chase was looking at the pictures on the wall and said: "Where is your Dad anyway?"

"He's at work, he is a firefighter so his hours are sometimes really long", she said as she finished her last homework question. Chase had a flashback when his father was a firefighter but then he came back to realty.

"Chase you ok?" asked sarah staring at him.

"Yeah, just thinking said Chase". "About...?" she asked. "My dad- a long time ago." said Chase.

"Oh ok said sarah"yeah said chase.would you like to tell me about it asked sarah. No said chase quickly.

"Oh, do you want to talk about it?" "No" said Chase firmly. "Well..." said Sarah changing the subject quickly. " How did you get your license again? asked Sarah. "I went to the Secretary of State's office just like you would so I could fit in with everyone." said Chase. "Oh, ok. Well - good" said Sarah. "I gotta go Sarah" said Chase unexpectedly. "Where are you going?"

asked Sarah.

"Heaven and then home" he said. "Ok, but come back please!" she said. " I will Sarah! See ya!" said Chase.

Sarah looked at her homework question and then back at Chase but he was gone immediately

Chapter 3 - Angels Demand

Jackson was sitting in the park as two people were flying a kite nearby. He thought that nothing could hurt them anymore because they were in heaven and he was in their dream land where people could create their own personal memories. And so, He sat down on a park bench waiting for his friend to come. Suddenly, he heard a noise and knew it was Chase. About time though Jackson as he looked up at Chase.

"Sorry I'm a little late" said Chase, "but I was busy and got carried away". he said, looking toward the happy couple.

"Yeah, next time leave before she asks you any questions..." said Jackson annoyed. "Her name is Sarah", chase said while almost losing his temper. "Well sorry, so- what do you want?" asked jackson.

"I need your help to find my father while I am away." said Chase. "Sure, but you realize it's going to difficult and will take some time. Not to mention that means being extra careful around Sarah." said Jackson. " I know" chase said as he leaned against the bench. "Don't worry, I will be extra careful and Thanks alot, this means the world to me" said Chase. "Chase, I know your father is looking for you, but if we don't find him, we are going to have to call off the search", Jackson said looking at Chase. "I know", chase said looking down as if in deep in his thoughts. "Alright and remeber, watch your back and protect Sarah" said Jackson. "I will" said Chase. "Chase- don't mess this mission up, or your going to end up like the one before you, " jackson said. "I won and don't worry, I am not attached to her but I will save her!" said Chase. "Good! don't fail the mission or I will have to look for a new angel friend!" Jackson said with a smirk on his face . You don't need to!" Chase said as Jackson looked up but Chase was gone in an instant. Jackson looked back at the happy couple and said silently: "I hope you don't."

Back to Sarah

"Hey Sarah", chase said leaning against the doorway. "Ohhhh Chase! Stop doing that!", yelled sarah. "My apologies," said Chase smiling as he walked over to Sarah.

"So, what did you do in heaven?" asked Sarah. "That, I cant tell you Sarah, its highly classified." he said as her face turned to a frown. "Well, okay then, I gotta go to bed now," she said. "Alright, see you later and goodnight, " said Chase as he watched Sarah go to her room to go change. A few minutes later, Chase heard Sarah's thoughts: "you coming?" Chase appared in Sarah's room.

Sarah was sitting on her bed and leaning agasint the wall deep in thought, Chase's presence was both disturbing and comforting at the same time, but to Sarah was more sad, confident and worry on her face to a problem "Are you ok?" asked Chase. Chase walked over and slowly sat at the edge of the bed and look at the window staring with Sarah. Sarah spoke: "Chase can you promise me something?" she asked. Sarah had moved closer to Chase. "

What is the promise" he asked. " Will you take me to my Mother's grave?" Sarah asked looking back at him now confidently with a look of hope on her face and mind

Chase looked at Sarah intently, he knew she was sad and needed to hear his truth. Sarah again went back to staring at the stars out the window as if looking for her mother.

"Why?" asked Chase although he knew her answer. "Because i would like to talk to her and tell her how I am doing", said sarah. "Ok, we will go sometime, " he said unsure if he would be able to keep his promise. "Ok, good-how about this weekend?" Sarah asked now staring deeply at Chase. "Sure" said Chase. "Great!" she said climbing into bed. "Goodnight Chase, " said Sarah. " You too", he said leaning agasint the wall and looking at the stars. Sarah went to sleep that night with a huge smile on her face. Chase left her hoping he could fulfill his promise.

The next morning Sarah woke up as usual, got dressed and grabbed her backpack and went to the kitchen where she found Chase staring out the window. Before Sarah can say "Hi", Chase spoke: "Hurry up and eat you don't want to be late!" he said turning around.

Sarah quickly grabbing her usual morning cereal.   Sarah

.t
.-

        ome on I'll drive you to school ", said Chase.

As Chase was driving Sarah to school, sarah was listening to the
radio. She didn't feel like going to school that day but rather to
hang oout with Chase and just do nothing. It was comforting to her.
But then reality shook her when the car stopped in front of school.
Chase dropped her off and said he'd be back later to pick her up.
That would have to be good enough she thought. "Thanks for the
ride, will I see you later?"

"You bet" said Chase.

The day was long for Sarah. Time seemed to stand still as she
watched the clock non stop. The day was boring like every other
day but when the bell rang, she ran out of school to look for
Chase. He was always parked in the same spot.

"Hey, how was school?"   asked Chase.   "Boring and very slow!" she
said. "I figured that!" he said as he watched all the kids pour out
of the school building as they flee on bike, skateboard, or run away
to freedom to go home or run from their bully.

As they got closer to Sarah's house, they both noticed that her Dad
was home early from work and there was another car in the driveway.
"Thats my Dad's friend Thomas" sarah said, knowing that Chase was
wondering about the strange vehicle.   Chase parked the car and
followed Sarah into the house as he keep his guard up to the
stranger.

"Hey dad, hey Thomas," she said as she walked through the door with
Chase right behind her.

"Hello Sarah, hello Chase!   thank you for bringing Sarah home!"
said Sarah's father.   "Dad!" said Sarah in embrassed as her cheek
flushed with color

"You're welcome Sir" said Chase. "Chase this is my good friend
Tom, Tom this is Sarah's friend Chase" said John.

Hello chase it's good to finally meet you and nice car said tom.
Thank's you too said chase leaning against the wall.

"Nice to meet you Chase, good to see you again Sarah!" said Tom.
"Well, it was nice meeting you but I have to run. John, I'll catch
up with you later?" said Tom. He left instantly as if Sarah and
Chase had interrupted their meeting.

"Sarah, how was school today?" asked her father. "It was okay,
nothing special" said Sarah wishing she had something more exciting
to tell him.   "How bout you Chase? How was your day at school?"

"I don't go to school but it was ok," said chase. Sarah's Dad looked disappointed and confused but quickly changed the subject. "Oh, well how's your car running? It sure is a beauty!"

"Thanks!" said Chase. "It's a great car and drives super smooth!" "Well, you can't ask for more than that now can you?" said Sarah's father. "No Sir, I guess not" said Chase, highly in agreement.

"Hey Dad, can I ask you something?" Sarah asked nervously as she played with her fingers waiting on her dad reply

"Sure sweetie, what is it?" asked John, secretly hoping it's not a comlex subject or boys

"Well, this weekend I am going to visit Mom"s grave and I wondered if that was okay with you?" said sarah playing with her hair nervously.

"Why do you want to go to your Mother's grave?" asked John in a worried voice as he turned his body towards her

" I just want to talk to Mom and tell her how I've been," said sarah.

"That's sweet, alright you can go, are you going alone or is Chase going with you?" John asked going chase would go for his sake on her daughter safety

"Yes, Chase will be taking me if that's okay" she said.

"Don't worry sir", said Chase, "I'll be there with her the whole time"

"Thank you Chase", said John. "I just cant bring myself to go there just yet, but I appreciate the fact that you two are going".

"Your welcome!" Chase said . "Sarah, I have to leave now, I'll catch up with you later okay? Good to see you again Mr. Anderson, and maybe I ll join you once you are willing to go to your wife grave but I ll See you later Sarah, said Chase as he headed out the door.

"Don't worry I'll be back!" said Chase in Sarah's mind.

"Honey are you hungry for pizza?" asked Sarah's father.

"Yeah, that sounds great!" said Sarah. "Great - give it about 20 minutes," he said as he made his way to the kitchen.

"Ok Dad," said Sarah. Sarah sat down and started to organize her schoolwork when a hand covered her mouth.

"Hey Sarah", Chase wispered. Sarah wad startled. She figured she'd be used to this stuff by now.

"Stop doing that!" thought Sarah. "Sorry, I thought you were used to me popping in and out", thought Chase.

"I don't think I'll ever get used to it, but I'm trying" she said.

Sarah's father startled both of them. "Sarah, the pizza is ready!"

"I'm coming!" said sarah. Chase quickly disappeared and Sarah went into the kitchen to join her father. There was an awkward silence during dinner.

Both John and Sarah were preoccupied with other thoughts.

Sarah ate quickly not really tasting the food and said goodnight to her father and made her way to her room. She was exhausted from a long day.

John couldn't stop thinking about Sarah's mother. He had missed her so much that he tried to forget about her. But his mind focused on his happiest memory of his wife and to finding out the gender of the baby until the tragic day of his life.

He knew that Sarah had missed her mother as well but didn't want to bring up bad memories. Sooner or later, he had to deal with his wife's death but he didn't think he had the strength.

The week went bye slowly as Sarah had anticipated the weekend. School was almost finished as summer break would come in just two weeks. Sarah had alot on her mind lately and school just seemed to get in the way.

It was now Saturday morning and Sarah was going to visit her Mother's grave. She didn't think this day would ever come.

She was sitting quietly at the table when her father startled her. "Sarah, are you ok?" he asked. John was concerned for his daughter. He knew she was going to the cemetary today and he wasn't sure how she was feeling. "Yeah, just thinking what to say to Mom," she said. "Ok sweetie, I'll be back later but please let me know if you need anything. You probably won't be here when I get back, but if you need me, you call okay?"

" I will", she said as her father left. Sarah watched her dad leave the house. He was hesitant in leaving and she hadn't been very talkative to him lately. He hoped she was okay with everything that was going on...

Just then Chase walked through the door. His presence startled her once again, instead of scaring her this time due to the circumstances.

"You ready?" he asked. " Yeah, you could have knock said Sarah". "Sorry, come on let's go", said chase.

As they walked out the door, Sarah didn't see Chase' car. "Where is your car? How are we suppose to get there?"

"We don't need it, we're taking another way," he said smiling. Curious, Sarah asked: "Like how?" asked Sarah.

Chase took her hand and said: "Close your eyes and stay still" he said. Sarah closed her eyes for what seemed like just a second until Chase said: "Okay, now open."

Sarah opened her eyes and found herself at the entrance of the cemetry. She was scared and excited at the same time, but she didn't feel anything or her body didn't have time to process it

"Chase, how did do that?" Stammered Sarah as she gained energy so fast.

"Let's just say we traveled through time," he whispered. "Wow", was all she could manage to say, as chase smiled to see the delight on her face.

"Yeah, you get use to it after a while and, its much faster than driving!" said Chase. "Pretty cool", she said.

"Are you ready to go visit your Mom?" he asked. "I think so" said Sarah.

They walked through the gate, not quite sure where they were going. They walked slowly, Sarah leading and Chase following. "You look on that side and I'll take this side" said Sarah. There was a lump in her throat and she thought she was going to cry. But she didn't. She had wanted to do this for along time and now she had to stay strong, but now finding her mother grave was the biggest task, since age been here when she was really little.

After what seemed like hours, but it was twenty minutes as Sarah came across the headstone of her Mother. There it was-

Nikki Anderson-

October 16,1967 to December 5, 2005

Loving Mother and Wife

Sarah was stunned. It was as if she had seen the headstone for the very first time. Her Mother died at the young age of 38 in 2005 when Sarah was 5. It seemed like a lifetime ago when she lost her Mom. Sarah looked up at Chase. "Can you give me some privacy? she asked.

"Sure" he said. He could feel her sadness and knew she was deep in thought. As he walked away to the other graves and feel it to see what happen to them as he walked further away to give Sarah her space.

Sarah was kneeling down over her the headstone. She could barely make out her words but she started talking...

"Mom, I know you can hear me and I would like to tell you I miss you so much and thank you for bringing my guardian angel to me! No one will ever take your place and I wish you were here, but between Dad and Chase, they have filled part of the emptyness that I have been feeling since you've been gone. So, thank you for that!"

Meanwhile, Chase had been walking around scoping the area listening to the other angels whispering about his father. Just as Sarah had been searching for closure on her Mother, Chase was also searching for the whereabouts of his father. So although Chase was here on earth for Sarah to help her with her Mother, Sarah was also helping Chase with his search with his father. They were each other's Guardian Angels.   The wind suddenly calmed down and then a huge gust blew and Chase's hair flew into the wind and the sun light touched down on his face. It was warm and felt good. He felt safe. He knew he was close to completing his mission here on earth but he knew his ego got in the way.

Chase stared at Sarah and listened in on her prayers to her Mother... "Mom, I know that I have been talking a lot, but Dad told me to tell you hello. I know he misses you but he tries very hard not to show it. He has not forgotten you, it just hurts him to think of you.   School is almost done and then I'll be in 8th grade next year.   And, you don't have to worry about me because I have Chase to protect me and I am doing well but I miss you so much it hurts."

Suddenly, Chase' head started to hurt from all the angels warning him that something evil is about to come soon. Chase started to walk back to Sarah. Sarah finished praying and before she could say anything,   Chase interrupted..."Sarah hurry up we gotta go!" he said anxiously. "What's wrong?" she asked.   Sarah was scared now, but sad she didn't get to finish.

"Sarah, we don't have time for questions - come on!" he said as he grabbed her by the arm. They walked about 5 feet from the grave when someone yelled out: "Chase"! Sarah turned around to see a dude in a black jacket with jeans and with blond hair with dark eyes. There were two other guys standing right behind him. "Chase - who is that? Do you know him?" she asked nervously. Sarah noticed that the mans eyes were no longer dark but now green and glowing. She was scared, she knew he wasn't of this earth.   "Been a long time huh Chase? What's the matter, you seemed surprised to see me? Did you miss me?" Chase seemed a little nervous. Trevor was evil. He worked for the Devil himself.   "Why are you here Trevor?" Chase moved in front of Sarah unsure of what Trevor's next move.   "It's simple Chase, I'm here to kill Miss Sarah, " said Trevor with a smirk on his face.

"You'll have to get past me first!" said Chase. "Oh, don't worry, I will!" said Trevor as he moved closer to Sarah and Chase.

"Run sarah !" Chase yelled. Sarah took off running as Chase kept his eye on Trevor.

"Boys, you know what to do!" said Trevor.

The two boys disappeared to find Sarah while Chase stayed to face the demon Trevor. If Chase could kill Trevor, his two friends would disappear. Trevor lunged at Chase with his knife. Trevor had just missed Chase' head as Chase bent backward to miss the sharp blade. Trevor seemed surprise at his missed opportunity.

Chase stood up and kicked him in the stomach and sent him flying backward into a gravestone. Trevor got up quickly and just smiled as if he was enjoying the fight eager for more. Chase jumped in the air but was punched in the face by Trevor. Chase retaliated and punched Trevor in the face. Chase grabbed the sharp knife from the ground and stabbed Trevor in the heart. Trevor screamed in pain. Chase did a chant knowing it was the only way to truly defeat Trevor. "sin ca le do di" said Chase repeatedly until there was a flash of blue light and the demon Trevor had disappeared. The human body of Trevor was still there but the demon was definitely gone for now, except for the soul of the human almost gone but it will go up but in the meantime slowly healing and not knowing on how he got to the cemetery.

Chase ran quickly hoping he was in time to find Sarah safe. Chase rounded the corner to find the two demon friends raising knife to Sarahs' throat. Chase had just grabbed the knife when the flash of blue light came and the bodies of the two boys fell to the ground and the demons disappeared.

Chase knelt down to see if Sarah was okay. He went to touch her and she screamed and punched Chase in the face but Chase yelled "Sarah, it's me Chase! They're gone Sarah, everything is going to be fine!" Sarah, still in shock sat up and looked at Chase and said: "Chase I'm so sorry, are you okay?" "Yes I'm fine", he said noticing she was bleeding from a cut just above her eye.

"Sarah, you're bleeding, hold still." Chase touched Sarah's cut and held his hand there until the open wound slowly sealed itself. He wiped away the excess blood. "Are you alright now? How are you feeling?"

"I'm fine" she said. " What did you do to me? How did you do that?" asked sarah.

"I healed your wound, I can do that but my powers are limited. "

"Thanks!" she said still in shock and unsure of everything that just happened. "I want to go home now" she said.

"Yes of course" said Chase. "Sorry about all this"

"Can we transport back to my house so I can sleep when you carry me home ?" asked Sarah. "Sure", said Chase.

"Oh, and I'd like to see how we end up there if you dont mind..." she said. "Yeah, I think after all that happened today you are ready!" he said knowing that it was a small thing to do for his friend. Chase held her hand and was comforted immediately. He knew that she cared about him and relied on him.

There was a flash of blue light and the next thing Sarah knew was that she was standing directly in front of her house. She saw nothing in between, it was a matter of seconds from the cemetery to her house. It was an amazing feeling! She could barely get the words out of her mouth.

Stuttering, she said: "That was awe...some!"   said Sarah. " You get use to it," chase said putting her down. "Thanks Chase-for saving me!" Sarah staggered into the house and immediately fell asleep. Chase stood over her, and whispered: "you're welcome..."

Chase was staring at Sarah while she slept soundly when he heard footsteps coming out of the kitchen. It was John, Sarah's dad. He had on dirty jeans and a black shirt. "Hey Chase, what happened to Sarah? Is she sound asleep...!" said John as he watched his daughter sleep more sound than usual, as he picked her up and brought her to her room. "Sarah had a rough day today" said Chase not going to reveal all the events that happened. "She was talking to her mother and she started to cry," explained Chase. John came out of Sarah's room. "So then, what happened?" asked John concern for Sarah. "I'm not really sure but she was super tired after we left...She fainted I think or something..." said Chase.

John sat down on the couch with his face buried in his hands. " You ok?" Chase asked. "Oh yeah, I just knew this would be a difficult day for her, thank you for taking her..." john said. "No problem Sir" said Chase looking over to Sarah's room. Chase could hear her heart beat in his mind. It was a comforting sound.   "John, um could you have Sarah call me when she wakes up?" Chase said as he walked out the door. "Sure", said John. "No problem".   John had a feeling about Chase but he put his feelings aside for Sarah.

Sarah was in a deep sleep. She was dreaming that she was at a lake sitting in a chair staring out into the water. All of the past days events had come alive in the water. Visions of her mother and the cemetery were overtaken with the evil doings of Trevor and the devil. The flapping of wings from angels grew louder and louder. Chase's voice was nearing...

Chase was standing over her disturbed by her dreams and he knew it had been a long awful day.

"Sarah...Sarah" said Chase in a gentle voice. "It's me, it's Chase and I'm right here." It took Sarah awhile to come to...

"How are you feeling?" he said. "Wow, I just had the weirdest dream," she said as she reached out to touch him to make sure that he was real. "I think you were in my dream" she said looking very confused and bewildered. "Yeah, I'm sure I was as well as some other people huh?" Sarah didn't speak, she slowly nodded as if half convinced.

"I need to talk to you Sarah" said Chase in a very stern voice. "Close your eyes and then open them again and think about home".

Sarah slowly closed her eyes and then upon opening them, she was in her room again, but this time she knew she was awake. It was a strange feeling to not know reality from make believe. She was more confused than ever and Chase had a serious look about him. She shook her head as if to clear a fog. "Thanks again for saving me Chase."

"You're very welcome", was all he could say knowing that he was responsible for Trevor ruining her visit with her Mom. Sarah was brave and getting braver every day. Soon, she would not need him anymore and that made him sad. He was enjoying his time here on earth with her. After all, he was there to save her and yet in a strange way, she was saving him also.

Hesitating, sarah said: "Chase, I hate to say this to you right now but I have some rules that I need you to know about".

"Rules? What kind of rules?" Chase asked "Go to sleep, I will leave you alone and I will see you tomorrow." Sarah quickly fell asleep again. As Chase left the room, he was upset with himself and the whole rule business. "Damn rules!" he thought to himself. This conversation would hurt Sarah deeply, but it would have to wait.

Chapter 4- Sarah rules

"Hey Sarah I am coming over..." Chas said into Sarah's mind. "Ok, thanks for the warning..." thought Sarah. It was strange enough that Chase could pop in and be visible anytime he wanted but the messages he could send just through her thoughts still took some getting used to. Chase appeared. "Hey" he said. "Hey there! Okay Chase, I wrote down some rules for you." she said as she held up the piece of paper. Chase was surprised. He figured after the day they had yesterday, Sarah was just a little confused. He didnt like the idea of rules. "Great!" he said sarcastically. Just flipin great thought chase. "Goody!" he couldn't hid the sarcasam. Sarah didn't seem to notice. She sat down on the couch and guided him to do the same. She seemed in good spirits and excited about her "rules".

"Ok, so - are you ready for this?" I mean to hear the rules?" she asked. "Do I have a choice?" he asked slightly annoyed.

"Actually, no you don't. Okay, just be quiet and listen!" Sarah was acting very bossy and Chase was not use to seeing her like this.

"Okay fine, let's just get on with it huh?" said Chase. He had moved farther away from Sarah, now sitting in the corner.

"So, was your death gruesome? Did you die instantly? Were you in pain?"

Chase glared at Sarah. "I told you I would tell you soon. But I will tell you, it was painful!"

Sarah looked at Chase wanting to hear more..."That's awful! Hey - why don't you like my rules anyway?"

Chase looked at Sarah and said: "My rules are way better!"

"Your rules? Ha - I'd like to hear those!"

"Just to let you know, Angels have rules and each Angel has their own set for each person they are in charge of. Therefore, I have a set of rules for you! Don't worry, I'll tell you next time I see you!" Chase left the room.

"No interruptions okay? Just listen and then we can talk after..."

"Fine, no problem." he said.

"Okay here we go-" Sarah said as she unfolded the paper

Rule 1- Before you pop in on me and scare me half to death, you have to tell me in my mind.

Rule 2- If I ask you a question, don't get so annoyed with me and be nice!

Rule 3- I want to know more about you, and I want you to talk to me about your past. Whatever happened, you can tell me.

Rule 4- Whenever I sleep, you can't watch me. It's a little creepy.

I don't do that, I just wander outside the house chase quickly said

Rule 5- I want you to stop being so shy around my dad and being invisible to him.

Sarah proudly put her paper down and looked at Chase. "Well...what do you think? My rules are fair don't you think? I mean, I just figured that these would help our friendship and everything...." Sarah was babbling. Now that she had said the rules out loud, she was a bit nervous as to Chase' reaction. Chase was spacing out and she wasn't sure if he was listening or not. "Uh, helloooo, earth to Chase!" She was waving her arms frantically. "Are you listening to me? Did you hear anything I said?" Her nervousness now turned into anger.

Chase quickly turned his head to face her. "Uh, yes I heard you, sorry I was just thinking..."

"Where did you go? You looked out of it!"

"Okay, first of all, I heard what you said. But then an Angel starting talking to me at the same time you were talking. He was reciting a poem I had heard when I was little."

Sarah was very quiet and looking at him to continue talking.

"Angles Of God, My Guardian Dear,

To whom his love, Commited me here,

Ever this day, Be at my side,

To light and guard and to rule and guide..."

Sarah had tears in her eyes. "That was beautiful!"

"Yeah, it is!" said Chase.

"Who said it to you? It's happy and sad at the same time. "

"Yeah, as a matter of fact she is happy and sad. She (Angel) gets to see her husband and daughter again. I don't know why that popped into my head while you were talking but I'm glad it did. And- I did hear your rules Sarah, I was listening to you. I think your rules are fine. I understand and I am good with whatever."

"Hey Chase, why do they call you the (Dark Angel)?"

"It's a little complicated. But, basically it's becuase I died a horrible death. When I went to Heaven, I had a hard time accepting my fate. I was deemed a (Dark Angel) because I was angry and confused and you are my first mission. Keeping you safe is my priority and I can't mess this up. Although we did kick some ass against the demons though didn't we?"

"Well, you're doing great so far Chase, I'm so glad you're here. You're my best friend! Did you just swear? she laughed.

"Is that all you heard?" he asked smiling.

Yes I did, but it's okay, You won't get punished or anything..." Sarah asked nervously for her angel swearing

"So Chase, are you ever going to tell me how you died?" asked sarah.

"I will soon! I promise!" said Chase.

"So, was your death gruesome? Did you die instantly? Were you in pain?"

Chase glared at Sarah. "I told you I would tell you soon. But I will tell you, it was painful!"

Sarah looked at Chase wanting to hear more..."That's awful! Hey - why don't you like my rules anyway?"

Chase looked at Sarah and said: "My rules are way better!"

"Your rules? Ha - I'd like to hear those!"

"Just to let you know, Angels have rules and each Angel has their own set for each person they are in charge of. Therefore, I have a set of rules for you! Don't worry, I'll tell you next time I see you!" Chase left the room.

Chapter 5- Angles have rules

"So," asked Sarah. "Tell me again why you dont like rules..." Chase was sitting in her fathers' favorite chair.

"I've never been a big fan of following them. They make me nervous!" said Chase with a smirk on his face. "Besides, I have enough rules I have to follow from the big man himself" he said as he pointed up.

"Oh yeah, the big man" she said smiling as she pointed up as well.

 "I only listen to the big man, my brothers and sisters, and now - you...I suppose I will follow your rules" he said.

"You have a brother?" she asked surprised. "I didn't know that! How come you don't tell me that kind of stuff?" Sarah seemed hurt and angry.

"Sarah, all of the Angels are my brothers and sisters. I wasn't fortunate enough to have real brothers and sisters growing up. Actually, I have a best friend up there, his name Jackson."

"You must have alot of brothers and sisters." she said.

"Yeah, but we just call ourselves brothers- and dont ask why!" explained Chase.

"Okay, besides- I wasn't going to anyway. " Sarah was lying when she said that but she didnt want Chase to know what she was thinking.

"Lying is a sin" he said.

"Busted!" said Sarah with a smile on her face.

"Sarah, on the more serious side, I need to tell you my rules so you understand me better!"

"Yes of course!" she said. Sarah was excited to hear Chase's rules, perhaps her rules and his were similar. They weren't at all.

Rule 1- Always follow His rules to the best of your ability.

Rule 2- Always pray every night to keep clear thoughts.

Rule 3- Stay on your mission and protect the one that need protecting.

Rule 4- Always strive for the truth and honesty in all mankind.

Rule 5- Always be with your loves one in Heaven but like me , I can't find my father.

Rule 6- Always be nice and respect people and angels.

"And the last rule Sarah, and a very important one is number 7."

"Never tell anyone that you have seen a Guardian Angel or you will lose your's!" said Chase looking at Sarah.

"I won't! I haven't!" said Sarah.

"I know and I'm happy about that!" said Chase.

"Chase, how long have you had these rules?"

"Thousands of years!" Chase looked very stearn. "There was a certain Angel who broke the rules a long time ago. We had to make some changes and banish him." Chase pointed down below...

"Ohhh" gulped Sarah. "I sure hope you follow all the rules. I'd hate for something bad to happen to you!

"Don't worry Sarah, I'm good that way"

Sarah wanted to change the subject. "So, school ends in one week and then I'll have a lot of time! We can go to the beach, hangout, get ice cream. Oh-and my birthday is June 16. We can have a party!" she said excitedly.

"Hey mine was July 22! Kind of cool huh?" A sad look came over Chase' face, he was disappointed he could no longer be on earth to do kid stuff anymore. Sarah noticed his sadness.

"You okay? You look a little sad."

"Yeah, I'm fine. So, school ends in a week, won't you miss your friends?" he asked.

"Well yeah, but I can see them anytime. No homework!" she said. Sarah was looking forward to a great summer with her new friend Chase.

"We'll celebrate your birthday together Sarah!" said Chase. He could stick around for her birthday but he really wasn't sure exactly how long before anything bad things happen.

"Chase, when you were alive do you remember your birthdays?"

"Yeah, as a matter of fact, on my 10 birthday I got a puppy and my dad gave me a ride on the firetruck!" he said smiling remembering fondly of that great day.

"Oh my gosh! That is so awesome!"

"Yeah, it was! Hey, your dad will be walking through the door in about 5 seconds. 4,3,2,.... "

The front door opened and in walked Sarah's dad. John came through the door and immediately sat down on the couch between Chase and Sarah. He groaned as if it hurt for him to sit.

"Hey Dad, how was work today?"

"It was okay Sarah," he said as he kissed her on the forehead. "I'm just a little tired that's all."

"That bad huh?" interjected Chase.

"Yeah, pretty bad!" said John looking at chase knowing the truth about him as an angel.

"I saw that fire on t.v., it looked pretty bad!" said Chase as he could feel John almost looking right through him.

"Alot of people were injured, some died today..." John hung his head and took a deap breath.

"So, let's change the subject. What did you guys do today?"

"Just hanging out, you know.."

"I helped Sarah with a little homework." said Chase.

"Good! School ends here pretty soon huh?"

"Yes!" Sarah said with a smile.

"Chase, when does your Dad return?"

"I'm not really sure, I think like a year."

"Wow, that's a long time."

"Yep, you get use to it! Well, I gotta get moving. See you later!
Bye Sir!"

"Later Chase! Thanks for the help!"

"Goodbye Chase"

And Chase was gone. Through his thoughts he let Sarah know that he
would return as soon as he could. Sarah could hear the faint sound
of wings flapping and knew that Chase had left both her house and
her mind.

"So Sarah, what are your big plans for your summer vacation? Any
ideas?"

 "Just hanging with friends, maybe a sleepover, my birthday, pool
 party and thats it! said Sarah.

"Well, I think that's plenty. We do have plans to go see your
cousin in Washington."

"Really?"

"Really!" said john smiling as he hugged his daughter. After the
long hug, John pulled away.   " I also want you to keep a promise
on the trip."

"What promise?" asked sarah.

"I'll tell you after dinner"

Chapter 6- John promise

After dinner, John had told Sarah that she would get to go visit
her cousin in Washington during Summer vacation.

Sarah was excited, she hadn't seen her cousin since she was two
years old. Her Dad had also told her she would be able to bring
Chase with her. Of course, Chase had heard about the vacation
plan even though he hadn't seen Sarah in two whole days.

Chase knew that when he was with Sarah, she was safe. Chase had
little time left with Sarah and he still hadn't found out enough
information on his father. He was spending alot of time with her
and although he enjoyed it and knew it was necessary, he was torn.
He had talked to his mother not too long ago and she apologized to
him profusely for his death and the death of his father. His
mother had missed him but said she was proud of the way he was
protecting Sarah.

He had kissed his mother on the cheek before he left to visit
Sarah. Chase appeared back into his car. Of course, no one had
seen him, but he had always looked to be sure. He started the car
and headed for Sarah's house.

Sarah opened the door and smiled. She was happy to see him. She
was always happy to see him. She gave him a big hug and said:
"you're back!" He smiled: "yes". "It's weird", she said. "My
dad asked where you were, he never asks that..."

"Huh, what do you know about that?" said Chase, feeling quite good
about himself. "You can tell your dad I went to visit my dad" he
said. "The one here on earth, " he said rolling his eyes.

"Hey- did you? ... "Yes, I heard, and- it will be fun going to the
fire house with you for the first time!" Sarah smiled at the fact
that he always knew what she was going to say.   "Show off!"
yelled sarah going into the kitchen grabing a coke. "Yeah, just
like old times. I've been there before, you will like it!" said
Chase.   "Hey, do angels do training?" asked sarah.

"Yes, I've had a little..." said Chase. "Oh, no wonder!" said
Sarah.   "No wonder what?" asked Chase. "It's no wonder you're so
weird!"   said Sarah smiling.   "Who's weird?   asked Sarah's
father walking in the front door.

"Chase is!" said Sarah.   John let on a half smile.   "Sarah, that's
not very nice, why are you calling Chase weird? Chase - are you
weird?"   "Dad, I know but he is sometimes!" said Sarah. "I'm
good with it John." said Chase as he glared at Sarah.

"Alright then, now that the weirdness is over, are you two ready?"
asked John. "Yes we are!" said Sarah as she pounded her fist in the
air. "Where are we going?" asked Chase. "To the fire house Chase.
I thought Sarah would have told you."   "She did, I forgot! You
know, with being weird and all." said Chase. "It's fine come on
son let's go!" said John as he stood up gathering his things. As
they walked out the door, Chase had a smile on his face.

As they arrived at the firehouse, they were all greeted immediately
by the dalmation who seemed very friendly. Chase noticed that it
was red white and blue. There was a firetruck outside getting
washed by all the Fireman.   "Tom, Grey, Danny, Nate, this is my
daughter Sarah and her friend Chase. Kids, meet the guys!" said
John. One of the Fireman spoke up: "Oh John I see how you are,

just in time to help us finish cleaning this rig!" "No no", said John. "It's my day off fellas - sorry about your bad luck!" "Hey Chief - you remember Sarah right?" "Why yes I do!" said Tom. "How you doing princess?" "Just fine sir, thank you!" Tom reached out his hand to shake Chase' "and you big fella?" Chase smiled and shook his hand, "good Sir, thank you!"

"You two want to take a look around?" "Sure!" said Sarah as she grabbed Chase's arm and took him inside. Sarah took Chase on a mini tour of the firehouse, Chase was impressed with Sarah's enthusiasm.

Sarahs' father stayed outside and talked with his buddies and then yelled in: "Hey you two, times up! Big day tomorrow with exams right?" Sarah poked her head out and gave her Dad a grumbled look. "Yes Dad, I know..."

The three of them said their goodbyes to the men out front and proceeded home. Sarah grabbed her books and said goodbye to Chase. "Goodnight John, thanks for taking me to the firehouse." "Sure thing kiddo, see you later." said John.

Chase watched Sarah as she studied and then stood guard as she fell asleep. He noticed the stars were particularly bright that night and left when he knew Sarah was asleep. She looked so peaceful. He wished he could feel the way she looked when she slept.

Chapter 7-Summer Begins

"Yes!" yelled Sarah as she came through the door. Startled, her father jumped back and couldn't help but notice the huge smile on his daughters' face. "Let me guess - school is finished for the year? Summer break starts perhaps?" he said. "You got it dad!" said Sarah as she motioned for Chase to sit down. "Oh yeah! Everyone signed our yearbooks, I cleaned out my locker and I'm good to go!" Sarah and Chase gave each other a high-five and opened up their yearbooks to read what some of their friends had written. John looked over Sarah's shoulder in curiousity. "So", he said "what exactly do your friends write about in there?"

"Well...stuff like: "you're a great friend, cute girl, nice person, have a great summer... that kinds of stuff. But as for Chase - the girls write stuff like: you're cute and hope to see you soon!" Sarah couldn't but help but make a face to Chase. Chase was embarassed and rolled his eyes as he glared at Sarah, daring her not to make fun of him again. She looked down quickly.

John smiled, remembering his own high school friends. "So he said, what are you two up to today?"

The two of them looked at each other. "Uhmm, I don't know? What are we doing today Chase?" asked Sarah. "I have no idea - I guess whatever we want. No homework, no school....the only thing I have to do is visit my mom and then after that, what do you want to do?" Chase asked. "Hum, let me think about it!" Sarah said, liking the fact that she didn't have an answer.

"Oh..." said John, "what is it that your Mother does?"

"She passed away sir", said Chase. "Oh I'm sorry about that, can I ask you what happened?"

"It's okay sir, it happened a very long time ago. She died giving birth to me, so I really never knew her but visiting her is comforting so I do it when I can." Chase "I'm sorry Son, thats difficult. You and Sarah have alot in common that way. Its nice that you two are such good friends!"

Sarah looked intently at her Dad. She wondered how he would feel if he in fact knew he was talking to a real Angel. Sarah knew it made her feel safe and she wanted her Dad to know, but didn't dare exose Chase.

"Chase, do you mind if I come with you to visit your Mom? asked Sarah. "It's okay if you don't want me to."

"Sure Sarah, that'd be great!" said Chase. Chase grabbed his yearbook and his coat and headed for the door.

"So, I guess we're leaving now? Bye daddy!" said Sarah as she gave him a hug.

"See you sweetie. Bye Chase - drive safe!"

"Yes sir! Always!"

Before she knew it, Sarah was at the entrance of a cemetary. The sign was ragged and read: Old Wisonsin Resting Place.

Chase did not wait for Sarah as she stopped to read the sign and observe her surroundings. He was walking quickly and had disappeared behind a very old (and creepy) Oak Tree Sarah found herself walking a little faster as she tried to keep up with Chase. She found him staring at a headstone:

Kim Archer

1860-1882

"loving wife and mother"

Chase stood there as if in a trance. Even though he was very fortunate to have had seen his Mother in Heaven, and had gotten to know her and love her, he felt cheated. Now, standing and staring at her gravesit, knowing her remains are gone, he wished she had survived long enough to have a relationship with him here on earth.

Sarah interrupted his deep thoughts. "Chase, are you okay?"

"Yes, I'm good Sarah, are you ready to leave?"

Sarah nodded yes.

"Sarah, if you don't mind, I'd like to tell you the story of my life here on earth."

Sarah nodded again. She had been so curious for so long, but had become such good friends with Chase that sometimes she forgot that he was an Angel. The thought had made her sad. She didn't know if she was ready to hear what he was about to tell her:

Chase - (human years)

It all started in the year 1886 in New York where I was in my room staring out of the window of the big city, listening to all the sounds, since he waiting for my dad to come home. My step mom Katie came home and had started to make dinner. I'm not sure what the reason was, but I think she had been planning to kill me for quite some time. That particular day, she was planning on taking care of me before my father came home from work. My dad was a fireman and usually when he came home from work, we would all have a family dinner together. But that wasn't the case for that day.

Katie had asked me to set the table and I agreed. I got up and close the window, and went into the kitchen. I remember asking her what we were having for dinner. She told me steak, which was my favorite, so I was excited. Then she had told me that my dad should be home in a couple of minutes. Seeing my Dad was the highlight of my day. Katie and I never really got along. I always felt like I was in the way and somewhat of an inconvenience. She was nice as pie in front of my Dad and he thought she was genuinely nice. I could see right through her that way. Anyway, what happened in the next five minutes, I would have never expected.

There was no steak - there was no food at all. I kept on setting the table, not aware that there wasn't the smell of food cooking. When Katie said she had to get something from her room and that she'd be right back. I was fine with that. The less time I had to be in the same room alone with Katie, the better. However, nothing could have every prepared me for what came next.

Just as I yelled to Katie that I was finished setting the table, she said she had a surprise for me. I thought that was cool. I didn't know the surprise was that she had a gun pointed at me. Before the look of surprise could come over me, she fired three times. The first shot was in my chest, the second was in my heart, and the third was in my stomach. I was really hot inside and I could feel the blood pour out of me. I fell to the ground almost in slow motion. Katie stood over me smiling then she ran for the window, I could just barley hear her yelling but to my knowledge, the window was close. When she told my dad what happen, she said According to her, she was in her room when she heard shots fired, and as soon as she entered the kitchen, she saw me on the floor and heard the door slam

I asked her why she shot me. She said I was in the way of her happiness with my father and with me gone, she could have the life she always wanted. She wanted a baby of her own with my Dad. I knew that had been an issue for awhile. My Dad had said that he wanted to concentrate on me. I remember wanting to fall asleep but I couldn't, I had to try to stay awake to see my Dad - he should have walked in the door at any minute. Katie had put the gun in the garbage can. "Not long now 'til your dead - Son" she said smiling. I called her a piece of shit and then I heard the door open. She yelled "hurry" as my Dad entered the room. I heard my Dad yell: "Katie, Chase, is everything alright? Oh my God" !

My Dad fell on the floor next to me and with tears in his eyes he said "hold on buddy, Katie did you yell outside? What the hell happened?" Katie assured him she yelled to the neighborhood and told him the same bullshit story. I tried to speak, but couldn't. I could barely get out any sound, the lights in the room were fading fast and I knew I was not going to make it. I grabbed my Dad's hand and with every last effort I had and tried to speak....before I could do that, my Dad asked who had done this to me. I tried to raise my hand to point at Katie, but couldn't. I was losing focus, and couldn't see much anymore, everything was hazy. I could hear the sirens from the ambulance, and then I could see myself lying there, bleeding. My Dad was crying, Katie was pretending to cry and the Medical Team was taking my pulse. I saw a bright light and heard a whisper that it was my time. I woke up in front of a white gate where I saw an Angel. The Angel told me to follow him and to stay close. I did just that.

"Wow! I am so sorry! I can't believe that happened to you! said Sarah. "It's okay Sarah, I learned that my death was planned and I have accepted my fate. I only regret not seeing my Dad anymore and growing up to spend more time with him". Sarah studied his face closely, noticing both the reassuring smile and the sad look in his eyes. "So is that why you search for your dad in Heaven?" She asked him, hoping to help push past this subject, which obviously bothered the aged angel.

"Yeah...and, um, the story didn't just end there," Chase said with a sigh.

"What else happened?" asked Sarah.

Chase tapped his chin in thought. "Well, five days later after my death, Kate told him what she did while drunk, but he said he didn't care. I remember this night so clearly." Chase closed his eyes and paused for a moment. "I remember, looking down upon him as he went to the front porch and looked up in the sky and said with tears in his eyes, 'Son, I am so sorry, but I'll join you soon' and then he... he shot himself... in the head...... and then Kate came home and yelled for the police, hugging my father dead body and she told them what she did to me and she was put in prison for life but she died three years later, and I'm sure she is rotting in Hell, where she belongs," he finished with a deep inhale of breathe. He had been talking on one breathe the whole time.

"I'm sorry," said Sarah, hoping to comfort her guardian angel.

He chuckled "Not your fault, but I think it's about time to go home."

"Alright" Sarah agreed with a bright smile. Chase gently gripped Sarah's arm appered in front of there house. "Hey Sarah, Chase," John greeted from the living room, sitting in the Master Chair (as he sometimes called it) watching T.V.

"Hey Dad," Sarah replied.

"Kids, I need to talk to you about something," said John, getting up from his chair.

"What is it?" Asked sarah as they sat down.

John took a minute to look at the both of them.

"I know chase is a guardian angel."

Sarah and chase were in shock until sarah found her voice. Ho..ww did you know chase was a angel asked sarah tugging her shirt. Because i use to have a guardian angel said john. Who asked chase. My guardian angle name was jackson said john as he watched chase face with anger and confusion.

Chapter 8-Secrets' out

"What? How did you know that Chase is an Angel? And - now that you do know about Chase, I might lose him!"

"Sarah, relax okay- I use to have a guardian angel when I was younger and besides, you didn't tell me!"

Chase intervened: "He's right Sarah, relax I am still here for you."

"Okay" said Sarah, still thinking how her Dad could possibly have figured out her secret. "Dad, how did you know?"

"Well", said John. "I couldn't put my finger on it at first, but your behavior changed, you were a little distant, but still in good spirts and always preoccupied. It was the same way with me when I first met Jackson-my guardian Angel".

Chase' face got beat red with anger at the mere mention of Jackson' name. Chase left suddenly without so much as a goodbye. "Did I say something wrong? Where did he disappear?" asked John.

"He went to Heaven" Sarah said wondering if he was going to come back.

(Up in Heaven) Jacskon was sitting on top of a hill watching the mortals down on earth. People flying kites, couple kissing, children playing when his thoughts were interrupted by the sound of wings.

"Why didn't you ever tell me that you were John's Guardian Angel?" Chase said angrily.

"Because I figured that would interfere with your job with Sarah!" Jackson said defensively.

Chase, trying to contain himself and his emotions asked softly: "So, do I continue my job with Sarah?"

"Absolutely, until things are settled, you are to continue to stay with her, Chase - I have accepted this curse to save you. After all, you are my brother. Are we cool?"

"Yeah, we're cool. I gotta go back and see Sarah and John. We'll talk later okay?"

"You got it!"

And with that, Chase disappeared and left Jackson.

(Earth) "Hey Sarah", said Chase as he flased back into the living room, sorry I left so suddenly."

"Geese Chase, you are still sneaking up on me! But, I do understand why you left, so no worries okay?"

John interrupted: "I'm glad you're back Son, how did things go up there? I'm assuming you talked with Jackson right?"

"Yes sir, I did. Jackson did tell me to tell you hello." Chase said, still trying to hold everything together.

"So", said John. "How is Jackson doing?"

Sarah interjected: "So Chase, are you still going to be my Angel? Are we going to hang out still? I don't want you to leave!"

Chase motioned to her to calm down. "First of all, Jackson is doing fine, secondly, yes Sarah-I will still be here for you until someone tells me otherwise. Plus, I know your birthday is coming up right?"

Sarah nodded her head with a smile...."absolutely, isn't your birthday coming up too?"

"Yes it is" said Chase. "However, we won't be celebrating my birthday. "I am a dark angel, remember? I don't have feelings like humans, no heart."

Sarah glared at chase with a stern stare which slowly turned into a smile. "Well, we will just see about that now won't we? Dad, tell Chase that we will be celebrating his birthday!" Chase looked at John empathetically. "Sorry, Chase but I have to agree with my little girl on this one, a Happy Birthday to you it is!"

'Thats' black mail!" screamed Chase.

John quickly changed the subject: "Alright - Sarah, you make popcorn and I will grab a movie! Go on now!"

Chase didn't look happy and disappeared. John and Sarah looked at each other. "Well that was rude!"

"Get used to it said John, the way I remember things, it happens alot!"

Chapter 9- Perfect day

Today is Sarah birthday and she is turning 14 today and everyone is excited and even chase, even thou he has to have a smile on his face to keep Sarah happy. John is getting everything ready for saran party until chase appeared. Hey john said chase as he put a pink and blue box on the table. That for Sarah asked john as he took a sip of water. Yep said chase. Good morning dad, chase as she hugged her dad. Hey how my girl doing said john with a smile on his face. I'm good and thank you for the bracelet, necklace and clothes dad said sarah. your welcome sarah and I believe chase got something for you said john as he pointed at the table with a pink box with a blue bow. Sarah open the box and there was a silver necklace with a square light blue inside the stone and little white color flouts in it. OH MY GOSH chase this is so beautiful said sarah as she hug him. Your welcome said chase. Is....that...the Vessels of soul said john as he grab the necklace. What's the vessels of souls asked sarah. Well Jackson told me that when a human dies that their souls have been kept in here but whenever you get hurt, you are healed by the spirit said john. Whoa so......ewwwwww there dead people that wore this said sarah. YES and its a great honor to wear and god made this necklace Chase. Well tell him thank you then said sarah. I will.....if I can find him and oh there mike said chase as he pointed to the necklace as the little white speck pass by. Mike said sarah as she looked at the necklace. Yes he was the 9 one to wear this and you are the 19 said chase. oh then so what are we doing today said sarah. Well your friends are coming over said john as he looked at the clock. 2 minutes said chase. Thanks said john. All the

sudden the chimes rimed outside but no wind. I gotta go said chase
as he disappeared. (Door bell ring, 2 hours later) Hey John Said
Chase as he stood by the doorway. Jezz son where have you been, it
been 2 hours said john as he had a Pepsi in his hands. Well it only
been 1 hour, so time different said chase. Well I guess and sarah at
the mall and don't even think about it checking on her and how did
it go in heaven asked john. Alright about 30 minutes later sarah and
her friends returned home with bags in hand. Hey girls how did it go
asked john. It was perfect said sarah. yeah and even cute guys
whispered lily even though chase good hear. Well dad were going to
our rooms and stay there till morning ok bye yelled all the girls.
Bye said the guys and they looked at each other. Do.. you want to
watch football asked john as he looked at the angel. Um k said chase
as he had one ear listening to sarah door. After they watched the
football game ended john went into his room and chase stood in the
living room to stand watch. The next few days passed after sarah
birthday, chase was standing by the living room window when the TV
went snow and heard the voice of his fellow brothers do some task
for him. CHASE yelled sarah. Yes said chase. Geez trying to talk to
you about five minutes said sarah. Sorry but I have to go away about
a week or month but I will be watching said chase. Ok....but text me
when your ok, about every 6 days and get back soon said sarah as she
hugged chase. I will and say bye to your dad for me said chase as
he disappeared. I will chase and good luck said sarah.

Chapter 10- Hard Days

Its been a week since chase has seen sarah, but he been
busy by helping people to get into heaven and saving
people. but he did text sarah everyday asking if she was
okay. Hey chased yelled jay as he ran towards him. Yes
jay said chase. Hey um about the search of your father
asked jay. Yeah what about rubbing the necklace around
his neck. Are you sure your father here and why is he
lost asked jay. Yeah I know my father here and he is lost
because he lost his only son in his arms when he died
said chase. okay um on a different related note um where
god asked jay. He out there somewhere and if you are
trying to find him good luck said chase as he flashed
out. Does everyone do that said jay by himself. Yes, yes
they do as a angle flew by. Well it just rude said jay as
he flew out. Well your rude too said the angle as he kept
going right with a book in his hands.

(On earth) Hey dad said sarah as she walked through the door. Hey
sarah how was the mall asked john. it was ok, have you heard from
chase asked sarah. No but I know that he probably busy said john. I
guess but I want him back here said sarah as she flopped in the
chair. Sarah you only have two days left until he comes back said
john as he put the newspaper down. Okay um I guess I ll go take a
shower then and then do you want to go to the movies dad asked
sarah. Yeah and lets go out to eat too said john as he went down the

hallway to his room. Dad yelled sarah. Yeah sweetie said john. I love you said sarah. I love you too honey said john with a smile on his face as he continued down the hallway.

(Heaven) Hey Jackson did you need any help asked chase. No I am good but chase you need to go back to sarah said Jackson. I will until everything is stable here said chase. It is for now, so go back and stay by your human until we call you back said Jackson. Alright I will, but let me help you with this and then I will go back said chase. alright let's go said Jackson.

(Earth) Two days later chase still didn't come back and sarah was getting annoyed. Chase if u hear me, please come back down, I am so board without you said sarah as she flopped down on the coach. Well I am back so if your just going to sit with a dumb look on your face or hug me said chase. Oh my god chase your back I miss you yelled sarah. You miss me asked chase. Yeah I did, you asked sarah. Yeah I did said chase with a smile. Good because today your birthday said sarah. No I my birthday was two days ago said chase. But you said your birthday was July 22 said sarah. I did and I knew you would celebrate your birthday and my birthday is on June 20 said chase with a smirk on his face. Sarah had dumbstruck look on her face as her angel told her about his real birthday. You lied to me Yelled sarah. Yes but I am a dark angel so I get to lie said chase as he sat on the couch. Sarah couldn't speak for 5 minutes until her father walked in.

Hey sarah...Chase you're back son, how are you asked john. Good everything fine in heave said chase. Good said john as he open a Pepsi. Dad chase lied about his birthday said sarah. John smiled and look at chase giving him a smirk face. I know that what my guardian angle did to me said john with a smile on his face. Gosh people can be so rude sometime said sarah. I know honey, I know said john looking at chase giving him a wink. Really guys really said sarah as she raise her hands above her head. Well you pass the test and lets see if you can figure it out or not said chase. Ugh I hate test said sarah as she layed down on the couch. You're not the only one said the guys. They looked at each other and laugh. Oh sarah grandma and grandpa called so we might go out there in 3 weeks or so said john. Cool said sarah. And before you even ask sarah, chase will be there too, so don't worry said john as he drink his pop. Okay cool and chase where are you going to be as she was looking at her phone. Chase is gone, sarah said john as he watch TV. Sarah relax and looked at her father and asked

do you ever get use to it asked sarah. Yeah but I am not
sure about you said john as he fell asleep with the
following of snores. Sarah looked at her father and
whispered maybe or maybe not.

Chapter 11-Over the Horizon

A cold wind rushed over Chase's fair skin.

Dusty, variegated leaves gently blew through the air, blowing
towards a nearby pond that last night's rain had created as a
light mist settled over the land. They rested on the surface,
almost seeming relaxed. Chase smiled bitterly and shook such
thoughts from his head. It was far from the time for fanciful
thinking.

The earth below him crunched and churned as he approached Old
Wisconsin Resting Place. It was a small little graveyard located
next to a run-down and abandoned church on the corner of a long-
forgotten suburb of Boston. There were a hundred, maybe fifty
more graves scattered in the field, although vines and moss had
overtaken many of them, and those that hadn't were weather-worn
and cracked. Just a bunch of meaningless people, who lived
meaningless lives, and died meaningless deaths thought Chase
grimly.

He had always wondered why it had been named Old Wisconsin
Resting Place when it was in New York. A play on words, perhaps.
Whatever the reason, it was why he searched for someone, anyone,
in the state of Wisconsin.

He approached the very back row of graves, to a grave third of
the farthest left, and brushed away some leaves, to find his name
engraved dully onto the gray stone:

> HERE LIES CHASE J.
> ARCHER
>
> GOOD SOUL, GOOD
> HEART
>
> LOVING SON, LOYAL
> FRIEND
>
>
> MAY HE QUELL THE FLAMES OF DEVIL'S CREATION IN
> PEACE FOREVER

Chase's breath caught in his voice as he choked back a sob. Here
was where the end of his life had been finalized. This grave
broke any illusion of life, for it was hard proof that he would
never get to experience all the splendors and even pains of life.
He would never again laugh with friends and family, never feel
nor give love, never get to live his life to the fullest, he

never really even got the chance to say goodbye to those he cherished...

He fell to his hands and knees and ran his fingers over the cold, hard stone, running them over the words, feeling the small cracks grind against the tips of he fingers, until his hand fell onto the ground. He gazed down at the dirt, knowing that his lifeless, soulless body was laying some six feet below, unknowing, uncaring. If he could just reach down and grasp his body, bring back life into it, he could escape this misery and pain...

"Nothing you do will change it, you know."

Chase wasn't surprised, or shocked in any way. Even if he hadn't expected him to come, he was too numb to really care who was watching him. Nor was he embarrassed about crying, for he had no more tears to give. He slowly rose to a standing position and turned to face Trevor's mocking face.

"You know," Trevor continued, casually yawning, scratching his cheek and glancing around, "I can't count the many times I've seen pathetic fools beg for their life, but if I had a penny for every time I saw a frightened and stupid little boy begging for his life back in death?" He took a few steps forward and glared into Chase's eyes. "Well...then I'd have a single penny."

Chase sighed. "What do you want Trevor? Shouldn't you be out reaping more innocent souls for your own sick pleasure?"

Trevor grinned sadistically. "Caught me on break. But I didn't come here to trade blows, I came to offer a proposition."

Chase's eyebrows shot up. "That's a switch." He crossed his arms. "Yet I think I'll humor you. What's with this proposition?"

"There's a lad. Alright look," Trevor approached Chase with his arms spread, "We both know it's impossible to cleanse your soul after death. In life, yes, but in death? Come now. So I offer you the Wings of Death. You can reap the souls of those whose time has come to a close and make a few... valuable friends on the way."

Chase gave a disgusted look. "You're a freak, and I find no pleasure in your murder. I'll redeem myself no matter what it takes, and that's the last of it."

Trevor gave a low, long sigh. "You can try and trick yourself all you want, but you are a smart man, Chase. I know your faith in this pointless quest has shaken. You are closer to reality, to the truth, than you realize. We are more powerful than life, than death, than even God." Trevor leaned in close to Chase to whisper. "All of it can be yours. I'll even help you. You're a lot more like me than you know."

Chase pushed him away. "Get away from me, you monster."

Trevor shrugged. "Last chance!"

"I refuse. You see, the difference between you and I, is that I am not as weak as you. The very nature of life, of living on God's earth, is to earn one's place in Heaven. To be given trial upon trial, and still remain righteous and true to God. I am his servant, and always will be. I will not be as easily swayed and fooled as you-"

The back of Trevor's hand came down hard against Chase's face. A flash of light and severe pain followed, and once he regained his vision he found himself on the ground, coughing and spurting. He hadn't felt pain like this since before he died. Angels weren't supposed to feel pain...

"You see now how far from weak and foolish I am. I came here and so compassionately gave you a place at my, at our side, and you so arrogantly and selfishly refused." Trevor unfurled his wings and floated feet above his ground. "I see the day before me when you beg for my favor, and on that day I shall laugh. I take my leave now, Chase the Black-Winged Angel, to let you foster your hatred and be corrupted by sin. Burn with this world, for I shall forsake and forget you."

Chase struggled to his feet, feeling shamed and angry having been so easily overpowered and defeated. As he regained his composure, a feeling of dread dropped into the pit of his stomach as he heard Trevor shout, "Oh and Chase? I should tell you how much I truly adore children!"

Chapter 12-Question unanswered

Feeling lost and, even abandoned, Chase found his way into the crumbling ruin of Old Wisconsin Cathedral of the Faithful, pushing open the small square doors into the prayer room. It appeared to be underfunded and lightly attended when it was still in business. When Chase looked up, he could see through the broken-through roof the Clock Tower, which was oddly enough still pristine, well-functioning and moderately clean.

Glass and broken wooden parts were scattered everywhere, including the door that led to the praying chapel below for the priest through hard time. As he looked in the front of the Jesus statues of he thought back as he heard the story on how the lord died, but he didn't hear the footstep of the priest behind him.

"It's good to see you again, my son."

Chase whipped around and found himself confronted by a very elderly man, at least in his hundreds. Almost every inch of him was covered in wrinkles and spots, with no hair to be found. Chase relaxed. No threat posed he thought.

"I'm sorry, but what do you mean by 'again'?" Chase asked.

The old priest held up a hand. "Ah, it has been some time now, hasn't it? Sometimes I forget that I am a very old man, but I assure you, I know you, and you I, for I was the one who baptized you."

Chase's stomach clenched. He was torn between disbelief at this man's ridiculous claims, dread at having to relive his past, and hopeful that he might have some answers. It had been about a hundred years, and there was no reason for him to lie. As far-fetched as the priest's claims were, he figured he might as well give it a chance. "What is your name?" Chase asked him.

The priest smiled knowingly. "Name's do not mean anything, they do not set one's nature as many believe, they are frivolities. If you changed your name to Henry Pumpernickle tomorrow, would you be a different man? I shouldn't think so, however I realize that we should have some way of recognizing friends from enemies and people from animals and pillows from sheets so I do not discount the minor value names place upon society, therefore you may call me Lainocik." He proffered a hand.

A bit perplexed and befuddled, Chase shook it, mumbling, "Chase."

A smile split Lainocik face, obviously amused by Chase's reaction. "Yes I know, Chase Archer, the Accursed Angel, the-one-who-was-meant-to-be-doomed, correct?"

eah but I plan on changing that lainocik said chase as he stood heir looking at the old man. Well good but do you what to know why he colt planed your death or why you decided to take the job from he Jesus or wherever the beard guy is said lainocik's.

"First of all, who is this cult? Second of all, why did they try to kill me? Third of all, if you ever disrespect my Lord and Savior by calling him a 'bearded guy' I will make sure you're life is painful and hellish and that you die a slow and torturous death," Chase ranted in long, ragged breaths.

Lainocik smiled menacingly. "You cannot threaten me, boy, for there is nothing in death nor hell that is worse than all the tragedies in life."

Calming himself, Chase asked, "Alright, old man, can you just tell me what all of this is about?" Its about the colt on why they choose your death because of the prophecy said lainocik with a smile. Then tell me before we waste time said chase. See right there boy in our world we have all the time in the world but when

your with your human there is not so much time is there said
lainocik. Chase looked down not knowing but what to say, until he
had one.

"Explain about the cult, because the more evasive you are about
it, the less time you have," Chase said coldly. He was through of
being played with. Now was the time for him to finally get some
answers, whether they were willingly given-

- you're a lot more like me than you know-

- or not.

Just please tell me about the damn colt already and who is
prophecy yelled chase getting angry. Well I think that we should
kill you because you are the angel of death and the prophecy
shell be completed said lainocik with a smirk on his face. Well
then here is god sense in you yelled chase as he threw the holy
water in the lainocik face. Lainocik scream in agony and hatred
towards heaven as his flesh is slowly burning off on the demon
face. Chase stood their in awe as the demon last flesh hit the
cement floor of the church floor.

Chase looked at the dark skeleton with dark mist surrounding it as
he looked the demon black eyes. Look at what you done to me yelled
lainocik. I am not the one who deicide to be evil and collected
souls and beside it's your time to go said chase. The prophecy will
be completed said lainocik. Before chase could speak he saw the dark
mist that made the room black and they crawled towards lainocik and
more angles of death came from above lainocik and grab him and about
to drag him to hell.

Chase was about to leave but lainocik last words stop chase in his
tracks. I will drag you and that little girl to hell and punished
you all to hell and your world yelled lainocik. Not today, tomorrow,
or ever because I will fight to keep sarah safe from danger like you
said chase as he disappeared out of the church. As chase walked out
of the cemetery he heard lainocik last scream as he went down to
hell. Chase looked up as he heard the whispers in heaven and nodded
and walked away leaving a firing blast of fire engulfing the church.

Chapter 13- Calm and Composed

Chase felt the worry emanating from Sarah through their mental
link, and through her, John's outward composer of trying to
keep his little girl calm, although inside he was frightened
himself.

"Dad, where's Chase?" Sarah whined with despair.

John grabbed her hand and led her through the house to the
kitchen, gesturing at the table for her to sit down. "Everyone

needs a bit of alone time, sweetie, I'm sure he'll be back soon," he replied, a bit anxiously.

"But he's been gone for hours! Usually he leaves for maybe an hour - max! Do you think something could have happened?"

"Honey," John said, doing his best to act calm and teasing, "What could possibly happened to him?"

"I don't know!" she yelled shrilly. "He could be hurt..."

"Sarah," John said firmly, crouching in front of her with a humorless grin. "That boy is already dead, you realize? He can't be hurt, he's probably up in Heaven right now, doing angel stuff?"

Sarah's face drooped and she looked agitated. "'Angel stuff'? Really dad?"

John ruffled his daughter's hair. "Sarah, watch your attitude."

"Yeah, she does have a bit of a problem showing respect, doesn't she?"

"CHASE!" Sarah immediately jumped up and ran to Chase, giving him what would be a crushing hug, if she had any muscle.

"Hey, squirt, how are ya?" Chase asked with a smile.

"Worried!" she scolded. "From now on, tell me where you're going, okay?"

"What, now I need your permission to go to Heaven?" Chase scoffed, sticking his tongue out.

"Chase," John said, cutting off any response Sarah might have had, :is, one, dead, and two, an adult, so he does not need your permission, little girl, but," he continued quickly as Sarah began to open her mouth, "this brat does depend on you a little bit, so a fair warning would be... we fair, wouldn't it Chase?"

Chase nodded, feeling his face hat up with guilt. It was true, Sarah had begun to rely on him, and he needed to make her feel safe, as was his duty. He felt ashamed at being scolded by a man who was, in all rights, younger than him. Although Chase thought, John is pretty level headed guy. T wonder how he got so wise? Chase suddenly felt a flash of admiration for the father. He must have toughened up from the loss of his wife and being the sole caretaker of a little girl, guiding her through things that he didn't understand himself.

I'm sorry," he said, suddenly wanting to earn this man's respect, "I should have shown more thought. I'll give more warning in the future." John nodded, apparently satisfied. Chase felt pleased.

"Where were you, anyways?" Sarah asked, her suspicious gaze raking his form for any clue as to where he might have gone. She found none.

Chase shrugged. "Wish I could tell you, but I can't."

Sarah fumed. "You can't, or won't?" she asked through gritted teeth.

Despite John's presence, he rounded on her. "Listen, what happened is confidential. Believe or not, there are some things you are too young to, or too uninvolved in, to understand. I will NOT tell you, GOT it?"

Her eyes rounded in surprise. "I g-got it," she said, her small voice quavering. Chase sighed inwardly, although he did not show it on his face. He knew he would have to apologize and make it up to her later, but now she needed to be forced to understand.

John's eyes darted between the two of them, seeing all and understanding everything. He had kept quiet, but felt that now was as good a time as any to intervene. "Hey, uh, Sarah, why don't you get ready for bed?"

She nodded and turned to the stairs, casting a fearful glance at Chase. She retreated from the room, and the two men heard her brush her teeth rapidly and jump into bed, her little feet pitter-pattering against the floor.

For a moment there was only silence. Then John broke that silence. "Chase?"

Chase gave an exhausted sigh and turned weary eyes onto the father. "Yes, John?"

John hesitated, then, "What happened? Really? You can trust me."

For a moment, only a moment, Chase doubted that, and considered not telling him, but then he remembered the wisdom he saw in the father's eyes, and how he had cared for him. All doubts were erased. So he told him. He told him of Colt and Trevor, of a future battle he expected, of the death that would surely come. He said all this in a flat, emotionless voice.

For a moment, John wasn't sure what to say. Here was a boy that was bringing possible trouble onto him and his precious daughter. But also this boy would protect them, no matter what. "Don't worry, son. Everything will be alright. You have people who care for you, and that's where you'll find the strength to fight

whatever battles lie ahead. I believe in you." He said this, and
turned, retreating to his own bed.

Tears brimmed in Chase's eyes, and he let them spill over. He had
never felt so comforted in all his life. But he had a job to do.
Wiping the tears from his eyes and smiling, he flashed into
Sarah's room. There he found her, as usual, dead asleep, and
snoring a little. Perching himself onto her windowsill, he
guarded her, and waited... and watched... and thought.

Eventually a shape slowly came to his attention and pulled him
from his reverie. The shape took form, and that form was his
mentor, Jackson. The young angel felt nothing. This did not
surprise him.

Jackson flapped his wings and floated inches away. "I heard what
happened," he said in a grave voice, "and I know it's hard, but
you must hold strong, for her sake."

Chase said nothing.

Jackson sighed. "I can't assure you of everything, or anything
for that matter," he said, as if reading Chase's mind, or as if
he ha screamed it in his face. "All I know is that the next few
weeks are gonna be hell, and you must find a way to cope. Must.
For that is your duty. You will be presented with hardships and
must fulfill your promise as a Guardian Angel, so says the Gospel
Christ. You will battle, and choices will be made. What choices
will you make? That is for you to decide."

And with that, he floated back, locking their gazes, until he
faded into nothingness, being swallowed by the night.

Chapter 14- A Time for Peace

        John sighed.

        He sat in his favorite arm chair in his den, downing a
        bottle of spirits. After everything that had been
        happening, he needed a drink. There was too much to worry
        about than he would have liked. Chase, and everything he
        was dealing with was rough, but he hoped it wouldn't bring
        Sarah to danger. He wanted to help the boy, but his first
        priority was to his daughter. That's what his wife, Nikki,
        would have wanted.

        Every time he thought of his wife's passing, it brought a
        hard lump to his throat. He tried to move on, find someone
        else, but he couldn't stop thinking of her. It seemed
        almost impossible to move on. He took another swig of his
        drink. "To you, my dear"

Familiar footsteps came from somewhere behind him. "Just so you know," Chase began, "Sarah is out with her friends." John slowly turned around. "I found out after I returned to Heaven for a bit."

Noticing the melancholy tones of the boy, John asked, "Everything okay? You seem a little down." Chase didn't respond at first. Instead, he made his way over to the window and looked out for what seemed like hours. Finally, he said, "When are you leaving for your trip?"

"Next week," John told him, a little concerned.

Chase sighed, then walked to the front door. "Be right back."

"Sarah!"

Sarah blinked. She saw Lily waving her hand in front of her face, desperately trying to get her attention. "Sorry, Lil," Sarah said, stretching and yawning. "What's up?

Lily triumphed. "I've tried to get your attention for like an hour!"

Sarah rolled her eyes. "Doubtful."

"Anyways, what were you thinking about?"

Sarah didn't want to tell her, but eventually decided it would probably be better to talk about it. "Just about many different stuff, I guess." She shrugged.

Lily leaned forward. "Like What?"

"Like the fact that I'm going to see my Grandpa and Grandma soon, all the way in California."

Lily leaned back in her seat and started fiddling with her paper. "Oh. When are you leaving?"

"A week," Sarah told her.

"How long?"

"Not sure, two weeks, maybe more."

"Oh." The pair were silent. It was an awkward moment between the two girls. Sarah feeling guilty about leaving her closest friend behind ad Lily not wanting her to leave but knowing that Sarah probably hadn't seen her grandparents in a long time. Sarah thinking that Lily was mad at her then getting mad at Lily for doing so, then feeling guilty because she knew that if Lily was mad at her for leaving it was only because she cared.

'So, how's Chase?" Lily asked, obviously trying to get away from
such an uncomfortable subject.

'He's a bit upset," answered Sarah quickly, "missing his parents and
all."

Lily kept staring at her, obviously expecting more of an
elaboration. "I mean what is he doing?"

'Well," Sarah started, scratching her neck....

Chapter 15- The days go on

Chase walked into the David J. Church, 50 miles away from
where Sarah's house was located.   Chase was looking for
an Angel called Afra. Afra was a beautiful Angel with
long blond hair, big brown eyes and very strong facial
features. She looked like a supermodel. She stood at
nearly 6 feet tall. Although beautiful, she was also very
formidable and had lost her Wings due to an unfortunate
incident 15 years ago. Afra was no longer an Angel and for
this reason, Chase desperately needed to talk to her for he
too was in a similar situation.

Chase knew that losing her wings was a sore subject but he had
to talk to her. Chase was approached by the Pastor. "Can I
help you?"   Before Chase could speak, Afra appeared. Although
still beautiful, losing her wings had aged her tremendously.
Chase had a lump in his throat as Afra approached him.
"Pastor, this man is with me". The Pastor left the two alone in
silence.

Years ago, Afra was assigned to protect a human child named
Zack, she had revealed herself as an Angel and put Zack in danger
and it had been decided that she was to lose her wings and all
the powers that go with it. Chase knew he was also in danger of
losing his wings. She was forced to fall to earth to become
human. Her immortality imminent. "Maybe losing my wings
wouldn't be so bad" Chase thought to himself as his stomach
turned upside down.

Afra broke the deafening silence. "Chase, what's wrong? I
know you didn't come all this way just to visit. I know I
don't have my wings but I can still sense things. You are in
trouble, aren't you?"   Chase gulped, "I put my human in danger
and I can't turn back, I don't know what to do".

Afra put her hand over Chase', "Tell me", she said in a
commanding voice. Chase explained that he have given Sarah

the vessel of souls and that the Soul Collector had followed her and her friend.

"Chase, I know that you did not mean to put your human in danger and I can tell that you care about her. You are forgiven this one time but if it happens again, you will be a fallen angel like me and your powers will disappear and the people in your life now will not remember who you are or the work that you have done. Now, leave this place and go take care of Sarah!" Relieved, Chase gave a nod to Afra as though they both understood each other. Each one knowing they would not see each other again and, if they did meet again, it would not be pleasant. Chase turned and walked out of the Church. "Take good care of Sarah!" said Afra, slightly envious that she did not have a human to care for any longer. Her existence, was now a lonely one. She watched as Chase slowly disappeared through the door, his movement made the windchimes sound a solemn sound.

Sarah had a look of broadness on her face as she sat in her room with nothing to do. "Why the glum face?" asked Chase. Startled but calm, Sarah said "because there nothing to do!" Chase smiled, having anticipated her response. "Well, what do you want to do?" "Hmm, can we just hang out and talk"? Sarah asked. "So Sarah, are you excited to visit your Grandparents?" Excited, Sarah said "Yes, I haven't seen them in a very long time and, they always give me candy or money when I visit, they totally spoil me!" Chase smiled at the thought. "Hey Chase, have you seen my necklace?" Hesitant to answer, Chase said, "uh, I had to take it back to Heaven." "Oh okay, so who did you see in Heaven anyways?" she asked. "I saw my Mother, she told me to tell you "Hello." Sarah smiled. She swore she heard the wind chimes outside even though it was a perfectly calm day. The two were silent as Sarah gently closed her eyes and fell asleep while Chase watched as her breathing became almost silent. A calmness took over the household. What they didn't realize was that Trever was plotting a sinister plan to kill Sarah and Chase. Trevor needed the Soul Collector and the Human girls' souls to gain his strength to rise to the ultimate power. Trevor would then kill all the other angels and any other religious beings.

Chapter 16-Trip Beings

John slammed the door to his truck, satisfied the last bag was packed and their trip could officially begin. " You ready yet

Sarah?" yelled John. Excited, Sarah yelled "Yeah, be right there Dad!". John heard the house door shut and looked over to see Chase walk past his Impala and head towards John. Smiling, Chase said, "Are you both ready to go?" asked Chase. "Yes, but my daughter can't seem to find her iPod - again!" "Found it! It was right there on the table!" John and Chase both smiled as Sarah came out of the house with her iPod in her hand dragging her overly large bag. "Did you pack enough stuff?" "Yes Chase, I have enough stuff!". "Good," interrupted John, "get in!" "okay, okay" Sarah coifed as she handed her Dad the rather heavy bag she so carefully packed. John winced at the weight of the bag "let's go! Chase you're going to follow us right?" John looked around one last time. "Don't worry, there's no threat here!" said Chase. John hesitated but trusted in Chase. And with that, John got into his truck and headed for California.

Chase followed behind the truck for two days until they pulled into a hotel. The small room wasn't much to look at but at least Sarah had her own bed. "Dad, they have a pool! Can I go swimming?" "Sure, just make sure Chase goes with you and I will be out when I'm done unpacking". Knowing that John had been uneasy about the trip, Chase gladly obliged and went to the pool with Sarah. "Are you going to swim with me Chase?" asked Sarah. "Oh yeah, of course" said Chase forgetting that he hadn't packed anything. Right on cue, a pair of swim trunks appeared in his hands. Chase had to admit that his powers were pretty cool. "Okay dad, we're headed to the pool", Sarah looked up and saw that Chase already had his swimsuit on. After all this time in knowing Chase, she sometimes forgot that Chase was an Angel. She shook her head and was pleasantly surprised on his athletic body. "Okay, let's go" and she grabbed his arm and they headed out the door. "I'll be down soon" said John as he stared at the two leaving. John was eerily uncomfortable but he wasn't quite sure why.

The pungent smell of the chlorine was overwhelming as the elevator door opened to the main level. The pool was empty, there was no one around which made Sarah uneasy and excited! "Yes, the pool is ours!" Sarah was giddy, life was good and at the same time, she felt a weight of anxiety rush over her. "Are you okay Sarah?" "Uhm, yeah.... yes, I'm good" she said trying to sound confident. Chase shrugged off her uncertainty "you first". Sarah made her way to the deep end of the pool and strutted onto the diving board. Sarah pretended she was an Olympic diver, "cannonball!" Chase laughed as she splashed him and then he jumped in. The temperature of the water was not as warm as he expected. Surfacing, Sarah gasped for air "It's freezing!" Sarah and Chase exchanged a glance and Chase heard her thoughts "he is so handsome!" Chase blushed briefly and splashed Sarah. "Race ya!" The two friends swam as fast as they could but Sarah was no match for Chase. "You Cheater, not fair!" They laughed for a moment and went to the shallow end. "My Dad is definitely not coming to the pool. I bet he has his pajamas on and is watching the news".   Sarah was envious, she too was tired from travelling and although she didn't want her time with Chase to end, she was tired. Interrupting her thoughts, Sarah looked up to see Chase holding her towel. She snickered "how did you know?" They laughed again and headed back to the hotel room.

"How was the pool kids?" Exchanging glances, Chase and Sarah smiled as John was in bed with his pajamas watching the news. "It was cold, I am going to take a hot shower". "Good idea, we have to leave early tomorrow morning, so get a good nights sleep". Heading towards the door, Chase said "good night". "Sarah don't forget to set your alarm". "I don't need to she said, I have a Guardian Angel, remember?"   "Good one" said Chase and he left the room. "See you in the morning" said John. "Good night Sir." Chase disappeared.

The hot shower felt good compared to the frigid temperature of the pool but Sarah didn't care, she got to spend more time with Chase and she felt safe when he was around. Even when he wasn't standing in front of her, she felt safe. She relished that feeling. She knew that Chase would always be there. She slept with great comfort. What she didn't know was that Trevor was looming outside the hotel room waiting for the perfect moment to strike down Sarah.

Chapter 17- Road Trip (Day 2)

The next morning came very early. It was going to be a long day of driving.   "Sarah, Chase, let's get some breakfast and then get on the road!" John yelled. "ugh..." Sarah moaned, just a few more minutes of sleep please!"   John shook his head, grabbed their bags and went out to the car. Sarah slowly got out of bed and grabbed her things. The three of them grabbed some doughnuts, coffee and orange juice and headed towards North Dakota.

The car ride was uneventful but peaceful as Chase listened to the radio and played on his phone, Sarah just stared out the window looking at the scenery and John just driving and humming along to the radio.

Surprisingly enough, the car ride went quicker than expected. They stopped for the night in Ramsey, a small town in North Dakota that probably wasn't even on the map though Sarah.   She was positive that the hotel was the only one around but her Dad made it clear that he was especially tired and needed to stop. Sarah was thankful, she had enough of sitting still and Chase, well he had to sneak off to Heaven. He had a terrible feeling most of the day that evil was near. And it was. Trevor had sworn his oath to seek revenge on Chase for killing his brother.

Sarah couldn't help but dream of her time in California. There were so many things to do! She had always wondered what Disneyland was like. She fell asleep dreaming of the rollercoasters and all the fun she would have. John slept easily, he was tired but couldn't sleep. He heard the basketball bouncing on the cement outside and he wondered who would be playing this late at night. He peered out the curtain. It was Chase! John stepped outside. "Pass it to me!" Surprised to see him, Chase bounced the ball to John and whoosh, he sank the ball for a 3 pointer shot. "Nice shot" said Chase. "I honestly didn't think I had it in me. So, what are you doing out here this late?" Chase shrugged his shoulders, "I just needed to think". "Well, I am here for you if you need anything!" John said as he put his arm around Chase. "Now, come on, we have a long day tomorrow, lets get inside." The two walked back inside to the hotel, not thinking that they had left Sarah alone and vulnerable.

Chapter 18-Live or Die

Morning came once again extra early but they had to keep moving so they could reach their destination. They had been driving for about two days until they arrived in another city called Chester, Montana. John had been listing to the radio while Sarah read her book. Chase had followed behind to make sure the trip was safe and have no problems, but he had a feeling that wasn't right so he send a message to Jackson to see if there anything wrong, but Jackson had told him there was no threat. Chase believed Jackson and let his guard down. This was a mistake.

Meanwhile, Trevor and Aero had been following the car waiting for the perfect time to strike without Chase' interference. They agreed that killing Sarah had to be quick in order to avoid Chase. "Are you ready Aero?" Trevor yelled? "What's your plan Trevor?" Trevor grinned, "I think I know of the perfect death!" Trevor looked down on the highway and smiled as he saw a semi truck roaring beneath them. Aero instantly knew what the plan was. "Perfect" said Aero. He had been patiently waiting for this moment and tonight, it was finally going to happen.

John was tired from the night before but seeing Chase in the rearview mirror gave him confidence to keep driving. He didn't like them being in the wide open when it was dark out. SLAM! Sarah closed her book loudly, proud of the fact that she finished reading the whole thing. John must have been in a zone, he had to concentrate on driving. "How was your book, honey?" "Definitely better than the movie, it was really good!" "I personally liked the movie". "Ha" she said, "that's because you hate to read". The two of them laughed for a moment knowing

that it was true.   Just then, a flash of light burst out of
nowhere.

Trevor, had killed the semi truck driver and the truck was
heading straight toward John and Sarah. "Let's go!" yelled
Aero, smiling as he could smell victory nearing. He would soon
have their souls. John could see the semi truck rapidly
approaching . He was confused and scared, he stepped on the
gas as hard as he could, panic set in. The semi truck was next
to them. He and Sarah had no idea what was happening and - it
was happening so fast! Where was Chase? Who was driving that
truck? So many questions. The truck ran into the side of
their car, rocketing their car sideways and forward out of
control. Trevor hit them again and again.

Chase was unable to move as Trevor and Aero had tricked
him by putting him into a trance. Suspended high above
the road, Chase woke up and saw Trevor behind the
wheel of the semi. "You'll never save them in time"
yelled Aero! Chase panicked as he saw the tiny car get
tossed onto its side, landing in a ditch.   Chase
popped into the semi truck and was face to face with
Aero who was obviously proud of himself. "Prepare to
die" yelled Aero. "Not without a fight", Chase yelled
back.

The two fought back and forth swinging their swords as they
charged each other again and again. Chase was no match for Aero
as he was still trying to regain his strength from the spell
that Trevor had put him in. Chase had never seen anyone so full
of rage as Aero. He could definitely use this against him.
Aero had taken all of his knives and swords and thrown them at
Chase. Chase had managed to get his shield and the knives
ricocheted back to Aero, stabbing him in the stomach. Getting
stabbed by your own sword was certain death.   Aero looked at
chase and spluttered out how as some blood leaked out of his
mouth. Chase looked at aero and smiled: "I guess I am evil like
you" said chase as he ripped his head off his body by using his
sword.

Chase could feel that John and Sarah were alive but he had to
hurry to keep Trevor from finishing his mission. Chase appeared
in the truck beside Trevor. Expecting him, Trevor punched Chase
in the face and started to choke him. Chase grabbed his knife
and stabbed him in the stomach making the truck swerve. Chase
kicked Trevor in the face, but Trevor's determination was
unaverred. "I will never let anything happen to them" yelled
Chase. Trevor smirked "you can't stop me"!

Using every bit of strength he had, Chase grabbed his head and
smashed it into the steering wheel over and over again. With
blood dripping down his face, Trevor whispered "soon, their
souls will be mine". "Never going to happen!"   Chase pressed
the gas pedal all the way down and steered the truck into a

path of a tree. Chase left the truck to watch it hit the tree, flip over and burst into flames. That was the end of Trevor.

Moving quickly, Chase flew down to Sarah and John. John dragged his body out of the car and looked back inside to see blood coming from Sarah's head. "Daddy! Where are you? Are you okay?" "I'm here Sarah, I'll get you out!" The passenger door open and Chase appeared looking at John. " Are you okay?" Chase said frantically. "Yes, but get Sarah please!" Chase got Sarah out quickly and placed her on the ground. She was not responding. Chase listened carefully but could not hear her heartbeat. "Come on Sarah, I need you to wake up". Chae started CPR, over and over but she did not move

John watch in agony as Chased tried to revive his daughter, he could hear Chase whispering "heart see moa soul hei sheia" over and over again as Chase held Sarah in his arms. John hung his head and cried. Suddenly, a bright light appeared over Sarah's lifeless body. Sarah was alive! Her heart was beating loudly. Before they could speak any words, the paramedics and firefighters put Sarah and John on a stretcher and went to the Hospital. "Thank you Chase, for everything!" John said as the ambulance disappeared.

Chapter 19-Coma

Three weeks had gone by since the accident .   John had been at the Liberty medical center recovering from his injuries and waiting for his daughter to wake up. Sarah had been in a deep coma with no response. She was alive but not awake. There was not much hope for Sarah. John was devastated.

The flapping of wings had startled him, John knew it was Chase. John could not find any happiness since the accident and Chase was no exception. "I know how to get Sarah out of her coma". Finally making eye contact John said "what are you waiting for? Get in there and help my daughter!" Chase nodded and disappeared. John wiped the tears from his face.

Sarah's lifeless body laid in bed as her friend brushed her hair. Sarah couldn't move her body or speak but she heard a faint whisper inside her head. "Sarah you need to wake up!" Unable to move, Sarah whispered back "I am awake, I can't move! It is so dark, help me Chase!" "Sarah, go to the light, turn around and walk towards the light, follow my voice!"

Sarah followed the voice which started to fade. Beep...beep.... she was getting closer to the noise and the darkness was fading fast.   Sarah heard her Dad's voice "Sarah, Sarah, please wake up!" Her eyes opened to see her Dad smiling. Nurse's and Doctors flooded her room. "It's a miracle! " someone exclaimed.

The Hospital kept Sarah in the hospital for testing and observation for another 2 days. She had made a full recovery. Although the Hospital Staff couldn't explain her quick recovery, John and Sarah knew it was because of Chase. "Where is Chase anyway?" she asked. "I'm right here Sarah, I'm glad you're going to be okay." "Me too" said John as he lightly kissed her forehead. "Dad, I want to go home" she said, "soon" said her Dad. "Thank you Chase for everything", said John. Chase nodded, "I have to leave for a bit, there are some Angels that need my help, you're in good hands here, but I'll see you later." Chase disappeared and the Andersons, headed home 24 hours later.

Chapter 20-Three weeks

Time seemed to stand still for the Andersons. The accident had taken its toll on the family but they were happy to get back to their normal routine. Everything was surreal. No one had seen Chase. Was he mad? Was he hurt? Was he in trouble? Even though Sarah had a near death experience, she couldn't get her mind off Chase. Reluctantly, John had to go to work, he did not want to leave Sarah alone but he had no choice. Sarah lie in bed, restless after so much time of doing nothing.

She was watching tv when the bell rang from the front door and she got up and opened the door to see Chase. She instantly hugged him "Chase you're back!" Chase hung his head "I can't stay this time Sarah". Shocked, Sarah whined "but why?" "I need to finish my training and because I put you at risk, I have to leave". Sarah looked confused and angry at the same time. "Chase, you would never put me at risk, I know that!" Chase looked down and then up at Sarah and said sternly, "I put you at risk when I gave you the vessel of souls, you will see me again though, I promise."

They did pinky promise and Chase gave Sarah her a light blue necklace in the shape of a cross. "Thank you!" she said. "Your welcome and you know what?" he whispered. "What?" she said " I am not a dark Angel anymore. Now, I am a Guardian Angel with different color wings." "Oh yeah? What color exactly?" asked Sarah. "Bright blue, just like the other Angels like me" he said. "Cool! Did you say good bye to my Dad?" Chase nodded, "I sure did! I have to go now, remember, I will be back, be good Sarah!" They hugged each other for the last time and Chase disappeared. Sarah looked back and saw a ray of sunshine where Chase had been walking. The clouds slowly closing in on the bright light. Sarah smiled as the front door closed.

Epilogue

Chase walked through the familiar clouds as he watched Sarah
watch him fade away into the sunlight. He turned to see Jackson
and they greeted each other with a hug. "Welcome home brother,
you have been missed!" Chase looked over his brothers' shoulder
to see his Mother and Father talking and laughing. "Go to them"
said Jackson. Chase ran over to his parents. His Father turned
towards his son and the two exchanged a hug for the first time in
108 years. "I've missed you Dad!" "And I have missed you son!"
The family walked toward Heavens' light together.

HE END :)

Made in the USA
Monee, IL
01 September 2023

41965596R00036